THE OPEN DOOR

THE OPEN DOOR

ELIZABETH MAGUIRE

OTHER PRESS • NEW YORK

Copyright © 2008 Elizabeth Maguire

Production Editor: Robert D. Hack

Text design: Natalya Balnova
This book was set in 11.5 pt. Bembo by Alpha Graphics of Pittsfield, NH.

10 9 8 7 6 5 4 3 2 1

All rights reserved. No part of this publication may be reproduced or transmitted in any form or by any means, electronic or mechanical, including photocopying, recording, or by any information storage and retrieval system, without written permission from Other Press LLC, except in the case of brief quotations in reviews for inclusion in a magazine, newspaper, or broadcast. Printed in the United States of America on acid-free paper.

For information write to Other Press LLC, 2 Park Avenue, 24th Floor, New York, NY 10016. Or visit our Web site: www.otherpress.com.

Library of Congress Cataloging-in-Publication Data

Maguire, Elizabeth, 1958–2006
    The open door : a novel / Elizabeth Maguire.
        p. cm.
    ISBN-13: 978-1-59051-283-8
    ISBN-10: 1-59051-283-9
    1. Woolson, Constance Fenimore, 1840-1894–Fiction. 2. Women authors, American–19th century–Fiction. 3. Americans–Europe–Fiction. 4. James, Henry, 1843-1916–Fiction. 5. Depression–Fiction. I. Title.
    PS3613.A348O64 2008
    813'.6–dc22

                                                            2007030221

Publisher's Note: This is a work of fiction. Names, characters, places, and incidents either are the product of the author's imagination or are used fictitiously, and any resemblance to actual persons, living or dead, events, or locales is entirely coincidental.

Henry is somewhere on the continent flirting with Constance.

—*Alice James to William James*
November 4, 1888

Never say you know the last word about any human heart! I was once treated to a revelation which startled and touched me, in the nature of a person with whom I had been acquainted (well, as I supposed) for years, whose character I had had good reasons, heaven knows, to appreciate and in regard to whom I flattered myself that I had nothing more to learn.

—*Louisa Pallant*, Henry James, 1888

It was said of her that she had never failed to win a person if she desired to do so, for her charm was potent and well-nigh irresistible. There were many who came under the spell and the spell was lasting. Endowed by nature with a passionate and even stormy temperament, together with a keenly analytical mind, she possessed at the same time such rare insight and tact, combined with a broad liberality of outlook, and had, moreover, such intense sympathy with and understanding of all forms of suffering, whether physical or mental, as well as all moral and intellectual aspirations, that she was able to draw out of people the best that was in them, while giving them in return the most inspiring and comforting comprehension. As her sister wrote of her: "She always helped people; knew, not only just what to say and do *but just how they felt!*"

—*Constance Fenimore Woolson*,
Introduction, Clare Benedict, 1930

What is hardship? A bugbear. Turn it about and learn what it is. The poor flesh is subjected to rough treatment, and then again to smooth. If you do not find this profitable, the door stands open; if you do find it profitable, bear it. For the door must be standing open for every emergency, and then we find no trouble.

—*Discourses*, II. I. 19, Epictetus

The work of Miss Constance Fenimore Woolson is an excellent example of the way the door stands open between the personal life of American women and the immeasurable world of print, and what makes it so is the particular quality that this work happens to possess. It breathes a spirit singularly and essentially conservative.... It would never occur to her to lend her voice to the plea for further exposure—for a revolution which should place her sex in the thick of the struggle for power. She sees it in preference surrounded certainly by plenty of doors and windows (she has not, I take it, a love of bolts and Oriental shutters), but distinctly on the private side of that somewhat evasive and exceedingly shifting line which divides human affairs into the profane and the sacred.

— "Miss Woolson," Henry James, *Harper's*, February 1887

Contents

Prologue

Mackinac Island, Michigan, August 1856

*T*he oar was a part of her. It told her where there were rocks and swells. It led her where she wanted to go. She felt the pleasure of her own muscles, working, as she pushed through the weight of the water, thick like cold oil.

She hugged the shore, rowing with the Lake Huron waves, instead of fighting them the way her brother Charley always did. With three strong strokes she steered the canoe around the rock she had named Hawkeye's Mark, into her favorite cove on the western end of the island. Here the water was calm, like a pond. She pulled off her shoes and climbed out to walk the skiff onto the shore. Like the leaves of a runaway water lily, her skirt floated up around her. With a heave she pushed the boat on to the pebbly beach and stumbled onto the thick mat of pine needles. Standing barefoot, she looked behind her into the woods. Then she unhooked the skirt, stepped out of its now-clinging embrace, and draped the heavy fabric over the branches of a juniper that lay on the beach, another victim of last night's storm. At least this time it was high summer. Cotton twill would dry more easily in the sun.

It had been hard work to row this far, alone. She was panting from the exertion. She raised her arms above her head and breathed deep to slow her heart. Her windpipe caught on the cool air, surprising her with a small cough. It was the gasp of health, she told herself. Not like the wheeze of death that had taken Emma. Then Georgie. It wasn't fair to blame marriage for the deaths of her two sisters, but she wasn't going to risk it. Give up her life for a man? Not her. She had too much to do. She hoped Mother knew she meant it.

Father, of course, would understand. He always did.

She reached for the basket that was nestled in the bow of the canoe next to the plaid throw and her boots. She shook the old blanket over the pine needles and sat down. Cora had made her a sandwich of ham and cucumber, but she reached for the peach first. She loved the wet fruits of summer. The peach was soft, overripe, but it had survived the trip. Juice dribbled down her chin as she bit into it. She took a long swallow of water from the tin container she'd borrowed from the tack room. Leaning back on her elbows, she closed her eyes. The familiar scent of spruce tingled her nose.

Overhead on the bluff, the pines whispered in the breeze. Down here, on the blanket, the air was still. The August sun beat hard on her face. She sat up. After all this time she still found it hard to relax, completely. But there was one thing she'd promised herself she'd do before the summer's end.

She untied her petticoat and, still holding it at the waist, walked to the water's edge. It felt slick and cool between her toes. From the lake, no one could see into her cove until they'd rounded the rock, that much she knew. She looked around again, squinting to see if anyone was in the woods. It was impossible to tell. But hadn't she waited long enough? She pulled off the slip, tying it to a branch near the blue skirt so that it wouldn't fly away. Ducking, almost squatting, she unbuttoned her blouse and pulled it off. Then she slipped her chemise over her head, and stepped out of her drawers. Nervous and hurried, she left them in a tangle on the pine needles.

Almost on her belly, she slid into the water. The cold shock of it against her private places filled her eyes with tears, but only for an instant. She kicked through the slither of weeds near the shore and made her way past the canoe. She could still touch the silty bottom with the tips of her toes, but she was, finally, immersed. With a little stab her bladder decided to release itself. The heat of her own water made her laugh out loud.

Birds answered.

She floated on her back and swam with her arms behind her head. When she stopped, her hands moved from where the warmth had been to her small smooth breasts. Treading water, feet flipping softly, she touched their pink tips, then slid down again to the roundness of her tummy, then below to the warm spot. Her legs opened like a frog's while she explored.

A cloud passed over the sun and in an instant the green lake went black. It was time to be getting home.

Squatting on the shore, she tried to shake herself dry, like her dog Buster, but it was awkward to move that way while she was hunched next to the dead pine. She patted herself with the corners of the blanket. Still damp, she pulled on the detested layers of clothes. A gust of wind reached down from the treetops and wrapped itself around her. Shivering, she took a bite of the salty sandwich to fortify herself for the row back. Despite the cold, she couldn't stop smiling.

Carefully she folded the blanket and wedged it behind the basket in the bow of the canoe. She hitched the skirt and underskirt into her waistband and walked the boat into the water before climbing inside. Grimacing, she pushed out from a rock that was slippery with green moss. At first her arms ached, but soon they became one with the oar, just as before.

Further out on the lake two steamers bellowed at each other. As she made her way toward the bend that would lead to home, she thought she heard laughter, voices.

"Connie," shouted a boy.

She twisted to her right. Two girls clutched the side of a larger canoe that the boy, nearly her age, was struggling to master on his own. They were heading in the direction of her grotto.

"Come with us, we have a picnic," giggled her sister Clara.

She paddled away from them, hard and fast, with all her strength. In her mind they were evil trappers, come to steal her, the half-Indian princess who lived in the wild, to force her to return to civilization. She stroked as if her life depended on it. Just when she had escaped the sound of their voices, the clouds parted. The inky lake turned to liquid jade in the afternoon light, rimmed with a fringe of pine. She allowed herself to pull up oar and sat in the rocking canoe, still and panting, with her face raised to the sun. She was alone. Safe again.

All her life, she would adore water.

Estate of Clarence King
Manuscript tied with blue ribbon
Auction Lot 24
Sotheby's 19–

Dear King—

Alice James once pointed out, in that fierce bird-like way of hers, that no one has ever written the magnificent tragedy of a friendship gone wrong. "Perhaps," she challenged me, lifting her little beak from the chaise on the porch at Leamington Spa, "It's just too difficult? Romance is easy enough—Tom loves Helen who loves Joseph who loves May, who's dead—but the betrayal of a friend—now that is a killing grief, is it not?" The question brought rare tears to her steely eyes.

And so, I have written this story partly in honor of Alice.

It is largely the tale of a friendship: a friendship made, and lost. It is not an exercise in finger-pointing or blame—which you know I abhor. But I take satisfaction, still, in getting at the truth of what really happened. Which is NOT the same as the way it looked . . . !

Sometimes the only way we can show how much we love a friend is to give him up. Or so Emerson said. Luckily, King, though years have passed since we've seen each other, I never had to give you up. And so I entrust this copy of my manuscript to you for safekeeping. There are people who would try to destroy it after I am gone.

Gone . . . it's impossible to conceive of oneself as gone, isn't it? Today I walked on the beach at the Lido, with my little Pomeranian dog Tello nipping at my heels. I tried to imagine the condition of not being—the waves lapping, the Adriatic sun kissing the tops of the buildings, the canals choked with gondolas, the piazzas mad with people . . . but no Connie. But of course in my imagination I was still there, watching from the heavens . . . just like one of those lady saints who sit by the Lord's side in those coronation of the Virgin paintings you so detested!

I suppose I am jealous, still, of what the world will enjoy without me. It seems I am just a small hole dug in the sand by a child's shovel, to be erased with the next turn of the tide. I would rather be a mountain, to stand purple and glorious for all time.

Forgive these morbid thoughts on a grey Venetian day. I ache for all that I will miss—but who is to say that I will have any sensation of that loss, once I am not?

King, you dared me to tell a new kind of American story—and always believed. When my modest flame flickered in the winds, you helped to keep it alight. And when my candle is extinguished, soon, I believe that, in your heart at least, my spirit will still burn bright. Thank you, always. Your affection was my summer.

Your devoted,

Connie

Venice, New Year's Day, 1894

CHAPTER ONE

Miss Grief Takes a Holiday

The story is in the journey, not the destination. Or so the philosophers say. But this is my story, and it has a beginning, a middle, and an end. Call me a sentimental lady scribbler, but my great-uncle James Fenimore Cooper—that most manly of writers—always said you should keep the reader guessing about what happens next. People hate to admit it, but all they really want to know is how it turns out—in the end.

My story does begin with a trip—the trip of a lifetime. I just never imagined it would be so short.

Mother and I had spent years living together in Florida, the perfect home for itinerant Yankee women in search of cheap lodgings. But it was time for her to leave. Truth is, at the end, I wanted her to die. We both needed to be set free.

We waited together in the dark. Old Billy brought another basin of water to her side.

"De ship's come for Missus W," he said. I nodded.

"She's going to sail ober the river Jordan," he sang, bowing his head. A flash of sun cut the room before the door closed behind him.

Mother grimaced and squeezed my hand.

"Don't worry, I'm still the strongest rower you know," I whispered. "I'll meet you there soon."

The hint of a smile tugged at her dry lips. She couldn't swallow the water I brought to her mouth in a chipped teacup. So I wrung out a cloth in the basin and pressed it to her. My tears escaped onto her cheek, where they joined stray drops of water from the rag. Outside, Undine and Old Billy sang.

When it was finally over, after all those dark months, the Wendell sisters descended on me like mosquitoes after a summer rain, urging me to stay in St. Augustine. Why not leave the boarding house at last and take the abandoned Finch cottage? asked Mary. It was the perfect size for a solitary female. I can still

see her left eye seizing up as she spat out the word
"solitary," just as it did whenever she complained about
her Yankee niece or the Negro maids who'd lost their
manners since the war's end. Of course, neither of
the two colored girls who worked for Mary Wendell
could have been a day older than the fourteen years
since Emancipation, so it's not at the feet of President
Lincoln that *I* would have laid the blame for their apparent misery.

But Mary was right about one thing. I did love St.
Augustine. Still do, but not with the soaring relief I felt
when Mama first agreed to plant her restless widowed
roots in its affordable swampland. One glimpse of the
Florida beach and I knew I'd come home.

We Woolsons had begun our family life in one of
New England's most water-starved states: New Hampshire. But ever after we were a family in search of a
shoreline. Father's work took us to Cleveland when I
was only ten, so my childhood water lust was divided
between the icy shores of Lake Erie in winter and the
summertime glory of Mackinac Island, on the strait
between lakes Michigan and Huron. There were also
grand interludes in Cooperstown, in the Finger Lakes
of upstate New York. In comparison to the oceanic
splendor of Lake Huron, Otsego Lake was downright

pondlike. But Cooperstown was home to Mother's people—and the link to her uncle James. Yes, those Fenimore Coopers. My literary heritage.

After Father died, Mother and I—her only unmarried daughter—passed too many sad, nomadic years, trailing through ravaged battlefields haunted by the ghosts of dead boy soldiers. Mother would forgo dinner to send money to my hapless brother Charley, who was seeking his fortune out West, but it was I who washed her failing body. And so Florida was a salvation, though not only for its prices. I came to adore its thick hot air that sits in the throat, so unlike the slap of Cleveland breezes; the snake-filled waterways where trees hang like curtains instead of erect Mackinac Island pines; the long-fingered palm leaves that never drop in autumn like the orange flames of Cooperstown maples.

Near the end, when the sun pierced the shades in thin stripes that burned across Mother's face, she had yearned to see snow once again. I was the one who couldn't bear to leave the hot place that had been so forgiving of our northern ways.

Truth was, amidst the confused Negroes and the redfaced heartbroken rebels, I had begun to lose my hearing. But the heat was a salve that helped me to find a voice inside my own head, to take the place of the ones that faded in and out.

And when Mother had gone, I was ready to leave.

I had waited long enough. Thirty-nine years, in fact. Europe called to me with the promise of a beau who knew exactly how to court a woman my age. Even a confirmed spinster like myself, with no use for a husband. Who earns her way by her words. I had been writing stories and sketches for nearly twenty years, earning enough money to supplement our small income and make up for Mother's gifts to Charley. Of course, back then I only knew what I had read in the monthlies and in books. There was good reason I was known as the premier "regional lady writer"—I was as regional and local as they come. But the friends who mattered, writers like Stedman and Paul Hayne, encouraged me to travel.

"You must be with fellow writers, darlin'," said dear old Paul, lighting his pipe in my bedroom one night, with his naked spindly legs planted on the balcony. "See the art, go to the cafes—stop holing up alone. You have no idea how stimulating it will be. You'll forget all about us and your local eccentrics."

"Get your feet off the ledge, Paul," I replied, slapping his knee. "I don't need gossip from the neighbors right now."

"Unless, of course, you'd like one of us to make an honest woman of you. We could marry, you know."

I threw a pillow at him, nearly knocking his pipe to the street below. He laughed as he tossed the pillow back at me, knowing how strongly I was opposed to the idea of marriage. As I'd told him many times, I'd never met the man who would be worth giving up my freedoms. How would he like it if I had to sign all his contracts for him, I'd ask.

And free as I was, I still had to manage my family. Easy for Paul to say that Europe would be the making of me—he never had to get there encumbered by a sister and a niece, the way I did. But my independence was purchased with the price of family approval and support. I was willing to pay the toll extracted by my well-meaning relations: transatlantic passage granted, as long as I was accompanied by my darling sister Clara and her daughter Clare.

"You do promise to come home, though, Connie, don't you?" wrote Samuel, the husband of my little sister Georgie. Poor Georgie had died five years after marrying him, though I always tried to think it wasn't his fault.

Of course, I assured him that I couldn't wait to return. To St. Augustine, where I'd buy myself a little house by the sea with all the earnings procured from my European stories. Perhaps, I wrote to him in my coyest tone, I would become the female Henry James?

What Samuel didn't understand was this: wherever I could be that writer, was home.

Funny, now, to remember how determined I was to meet him. Hellbent, I believe the boy adventure writers would say. Consumed by an *idée fixe*, as Harry himself might put it, with his weakness for the French *bon mot*. Yes, I was as obsessed as many of the heroines of my stories, like poor "Miss Grief," who desperately seeks the help of the pompous male writer whose every word she has memorized. Miss Grief arrives every night in her threadbare clothes at the home of her favorite writer, just to beg him to read her manuscript. Of course, the difference is that I was so well published, a critic in *The Nation* had accused me of "infesting the magazines," and Miss Grief died without a word seeing print. But I knew how she felt. The male geniuses were contemptuous of us both—we were the dreaded lady scribblers.

I created Miss Grief, and so I knew her heart's desire: communion with an artist she admired. More than his connections, his edits—his snide, contemptuous edits—she wanted to talk to him, to be appreciated by him. She wanted his friendship. And so it was for me.

You see, when it came to Harry, I was not interested in the man—another man. What compelled me was the writer.

Have you ever been heartbroken to finish a book? Has a writer kept whispering in your ear long after the last page is turned? Did you ever long to meet that person who sees the world with your eyes, so that you can continue the conversation?

That is how I felt about Harry, before I ever laid eyes on him.

Mr. Howells spared no criticism of my stories whenever he accepted one for his magazine, but he and I agreed on this one point. Henry James was doing something totally new. He brought characters, their mental processes, alive on the page, without having them do anything at all! It was the most remarkable of feats.

And so, in the middle of life, I did what few women do. Just nine months after Mother died, I set off on my own—to find him.

CHAPTER TWO

The Americans

$\mathscr{A}$nticipation makes me hungry. And so at sea, I was famished. The crossing was so violent, the most seasoned passengers kept to their cabins. But born with "fins instead of legs," as Father used to say, I took my seat in the dining room for every meal, often to find myself the sole person at our table. Perhaps with my sailor's stomach I should have sought out a lucrative career as a chronicler of shipboard society for the papers . . . but the future didn't hold much for me in the way of ocean life. A gypsy fortuneteller spying this American "she-novelist," huddled on the deck in a horsehair blanket, would have predicted what I couldn't know then: I would never cross the Atlantic again.

On that maiden voyage in December of 1879, I must have been a peculiar sight: a forty-year-old woman as agitated and hungry as a ten-year-old boy, helping herself to second portions of roast beef and wine and custard as the ship rolled back and forth. Truth is, I was glad for the chance to contemplate my future alone, staring at the grey horizon while my sister and niece moaned in their beds. Selfish, but inescapable—I preferred my own company to the strain of making small talk with the Clara-belles. I scribbled in my cabin, munching on biscuits while water dashed the porthole and the lamp waved on its hook. It was a peculiar kind of heaven.

After the ordeal of the journey it was hard for the girls to find a Liverpool that was encased in a sheet of ice. But London greeted us with a cozy Mayfair fireplace and enough cold-weather entertainments to keep them busy. For two weeks I was a well-behaved sister and auntie, putting social engagements ahead of viewing the art, or even my own writing—until one cold, frantic day that ended in a tedious dinner with neighbors of our Cooperstown cousins. Every one of them had affected a ridiculous imitation of British pronunciation, after only two months abroad! Was this the fellowship for which I had waited forty long years?

In the carriage afterward, I lost my temper. "Do you have so little regard for me that I am granted less control of my time and my company than a sixteen-year-old girl on holiday would have the right to expect?" I hissed at Clara. She burst into tears.

In our hotel I sat her down by the fireplace and we negotiated like statesmen. Father would have been proud of my diplomatic skills. We hashed out the compromise that would keep me sane, if not overjoyed: older sister Connie was not available for touring between 7 a.m. and 1 in the afternoon. Nor would she be expected to go out every evening. Nothing fills me with more dread, even now, than the prospect of a fixed social appointment, hanging like an owl over my work. And large groups fill me with despair. I would gladly give up twenty dinner parties for one real conversation with a friend.

My fit only confirmed Clara's ideas that I was a moody and variable creature, who needed to be handled with care. Good for me. At least as her "artistic" older sister I would enjoy greater freedom than your average maiden lady.

Poor Clara. She had no idea what consumed me. I was not in England to tour the blood-stained Tower of London or to visit acquaintances of acquaintances of acquaintances. I was there to create my new life. Among my private papers I had stashed a letter of introduction to Henry James, which I'd begged off his cousin Henrietta Pell-Clark when I met her in Cooperstown the month before we sailed. Why else did everyone think I had traveled to upstate New York as winter set in? For the joy of freezing my toes while sledding on frozen hills? No, I returned to Uncle Fenimore's home in the snow, to secure that d__ letter.

Late in the evening, when the clip-clop of carriage horses had abated and I was sitting in my chair, reading by lamplight, I would extract the precious letter from the back of my journal and press it to my cheek. Save me from these fools, I murmured, knowing that soon I'd receive a response to the note I'd left with James's butler.

The day I discovered he was in Paris and not planning to return from the continent before Christmas, the world went black.

Clara was alarmed to see my spirits sink. "But Connie," she said with that desperately chirpy voice, like a canary that's been hit in the head, "you are such a well-known authoress already. Why do you fret so over meeting another one?"

I could not bear to listen to her. With a moan I sent her off to ring for tea and biscuits—knowing she'd feel useful if she provided the dull fare that is supposed to calm female nerves.

That night I lay in the dark, thrashing. The throb in my bad ear threatened to explode. Only by composing myself would I calm the pain. And discover where to find the object of my quest.

The next day I resolved to begin our icy journey through France as soon as the new year came.

The cool stony elegance of Florence sits like a cut jewel against the velvet hills that surround her. At last, I was breathing the old world, the old culture, in a way that was never true in England or even in the south of France. The funny Florentine churches with their pasted-on fronts of marble were another matter—I confess they confused me. But I reread Harry's *Transatlantic Sketches* and kept studying the paintings, sitting alone before them, so that I would be ready to meet him.

It was no easy task. At a tea with various American wives and dowagers I was warned that Mr. James had no interest in meeting a certain lady novelist from Florida. He actually told someone that a Miss Woolson was chasing him across Europe! All because when I discovered he had left Paris, I went to great lengths to ensure that my letter was forwarded to his Florence address . . . His success had made him so popular, he maintained, that he had to devote an hour a day just to reviewing his invitations and engagements. There was no time to meet second-rate regional scribblers.

Remember, these were still the early days, just after *Daisy Miller.* In those salad days of acclaim, when his hostility to lady novelists was green and fierce, he wouldn't have even cared to learn that I had been the anonymous reviewer of *The Europeans* in the *Atlantic Monthly.* What would matter was my literary pedigree. So, like any woman, I used what I had.

When a friend of Clara's, Miss Celia Gordon, mentioned that she would be dining with the young master, I saw my opening. Would she please regale the busy Mr. James with tales of my relation to great uncle James Fenimore Cooper? As I cut her another piece of almond torte, I fed her the story of how Clara and I had discovered at a small local library a Cooper book unknown to us—*Excursions in Italy,* the story of the family's sojourn in a villa outside the city fifty years before our own visit. As I expected, the social Bostonian changed his tune. Two days after the dinner he dashed me a note saying that he was eager to meet the "living link to the literary frontier of America!"

And wouldn't Uncle Fenimore have laughed at the sight of this peculiar creature when he finally came to call.

A tall, bearded man stood still like a column of grey silk amidst the chaos of our parlor at Madame Barbensi's pensione on the Lung'Arno. Only his face moved, and from its expression I thought he had caught wind of something slightly off, like a day-old fish. His pale eyes seemed to slide off center, like marbles on a slant table, though if one followed his gaze it led to the figure of the seventeen-year-old porter Tito carrying the trunks of a departing family to the carriage outside. Thinking the sight of such mundane labors disgusted him, I rushed to the great writer's side.

He looked me up and down with some bafflement, as if he weren't quite sure what I was doing there. "Miss Constance Fenimore Woolson?"

"Yes, Mr. James. I am so delighted to meet you, at last. I feel as if I've known you through your writings for years now."

He blinked again. Had he expected me to be wearing leather stockings and carrying a rifle?

"Miss Woolson, any friend of my cousin Henrietta and her dear departed sister is someone with whom I am eager to share the pleasures of a Tuscan afternoon." He patted his eyes with the square of linen he pulled from his vest pocket, like a clergyman officiating at a funeral. "Henrietta spoke of you so warmly. Her sister Minny was an angel. Did you know her well?"

This was rich, I thought. Everyone in Cooperstown knew that cousin Henry didn't answer any of the dying Minny's letters in the last months of her life. His silence, interpreted as coldness, had broken the consumptive girl's heart in her final days. But I remembered Father and how much I still talked to him in my dreams.

"Some live more vibrantly after death than they did in life," I answered. "Our imaginations round them and give them enduring form, like sculpture. It's a kind of immortality."

"Exactly!" He clasped my hand, not yet gloved, and I felt the soft dampness of his palm.

"In fact," I continued, "I find that the characters in my mind, whether real or imagined, behave much more sympathetically than do characters in everyday life. Just think how many cups of tea you and I have already shared in my imagination."

For a second, he stiffened. Then I smiled and he let loose a single laugh that was something like the bark of a small dog.

Leaning forward with an awkward tilt of his spine, as if he were about to make an illicit proposition, Henry James said in a near whisper, "Miss Woolson, have you ever been to the Uffizi?"

Henry James made me his project over the next few weeks. By his side, I saw many beautiful pictures. He tried to make me see as he saw. In this, he was like most men. But in other ways he was completely new—a fountain from which I never wanted to stop drinking. I wanted to think and feel as the artist in him did. An impossible task, it turned out, though I did lose some of my aversion to those sad-eyed monks of Giotto.

He especially loved the statues of Michelangelo. Once he discovered that the male nude did not make me faint, the Academia became a regular stop. I never enjoyed David as much as he did. Of course, I couldn't confess to Harry, then, that I knew the perfect chiseled figure bore little relation to the soft and slippery shapes of real men, in all their mottled, furry glory. The same was true at the Medici Chapel, where, despite their overdeveloped muscles, the statues writhed with a kind of agony I could only attribute to their creator's state of mind.

"These fellows look exhausted," I said one afternoon, standing in front of the reclining figures named "Day" and "Night." "In fact, it seems to me that Mr. Michelangelo has worked these poor models to death. This one over here looks like our porter Tito when he staggers home after a night of debauchery, just as I am taking my morning walk."

"The exhaustion of passion spent, indeed, Miss Woolson," he trembled. "But then—!" Overcome, he strutted off to calm himself by staring at a patch of inlaid floor, whether because of my ignorance or because he was imagining Tito in the throes of debauchery, I'm still not certain.

Afterward, we made our way to the Piazza della Signoria. He lowered himself with deliberate caution onto a small filigree iron chair at Doney's Café. He was too large, really, to sit comfortably in most Italian café furniture. I wasn't yet accustomed to his pale complexion, which made him look underbaked. He sipped strong coffee out of a porcelain cup so tiny he could barely hold it in his doughy fingers.

"This is such a stern piazza—more history than beauty," I said. Henry's eye followed a group of French tourists who were headed for the Loggia dei Lanzi and its strange assortment of sculptures. I licked a drop of pastry cream off my spoon. His raised eyebrow suggested I had done something as risqué as displaying my knee.

I shrugged. "I love these Italian creams. There's nothing like them at home."

"Home," he intoned with a round British-sounding vowel. "And exactly where do you consider home to be, Miss Woolson?"

"That's a good question, Mr. James. I have lived in many places, from New Hampshire to Ohio to Florida. But for someone who is not attached to anything but her work, like myself, home is where the imagination flowers. Where the writing can be done." I wanted to say, home is where I can make a friend, a soulmate, out of someone like you.

"Miss Woolson, I find it difficult to believe there is no Michigan suitor waiting for you, the authoress of such wonderful tales of the Great Lakes, to return?"

"Ha! Can you imagine how awful that would be? Bursting out of his waistcoat, wanting me to be sure that the cook fixes his chop just so?" I chuckled with a start that nearly tipped over my lemonade. "Then I would surely lose my mind."

"No deerslayer then for you, Miss Woolson? Some burly frontier man ready to hunt your supper every day, returning home at night with an animal slung across his broad and manly shoulders?" He giggled at the idea.

"Clearly you've never had to prepare and skin and hang a fresh-killed animal, Mr. James, or you wouldn't consider it so delightful. I'd rather catch my own fish, thank you very much."

"Do you really mean to tell me, Miss Woolson, that you don't long for the wedded bliss of our compatriots over there?" he asked. A flush of mischief burned his bready cheeks.

I followed the tilt of his jaw to a middle-aged couple who were arguing several yards away. The gentleman, whose plaid jacket pulled so tight beneath his arms he seemed to be stitched into his clothes, was pleading with a short trim woman in bright blue, who clutched a *Baedaker* to her chest. We couldn't hear their words, only the flat vowel sounds that rose and fell in the unmistakable sputtering rhythm of our native land.

"Apparently the husband is imploring his wife to leave the paintings aside and take some tea," observed my companion.

"I'm not so certain. Perhaps he is begging this lady to return to the hotel for an assignation while his wife is safely away on an expedition to Siena with her sister," I replied with a wink.

He grinned. "Or, better yet—she has renounced her family fortune for him—the divorced Casanova of Pittsburgh—and he is imploring her to reconsider, as it was a point of attraction far more compelling than her taste in touring suits, or even, *faux de mieux*, her hats."

We were laughing so hard that I began to choke. Harry covered his eyes with his napkin, but his shoulders continued to shake. I looked at him, giggling behind his napkin, and thought, Henry James is laughing, with me!

I took another gulp of lemonade. "Mr. James, if anyone should hear us—"

"Never mind, Miss Woolson. We are free here in Europe, where artists—especially American artists—are forgiven many sins."

Our imaginary friends left the piazza, the man scurrying after his determined female companion. "It's true that European society is more relaxed in certain respects, particularly for older women," I agreed, "though I suspect the native girls live very circumscribed lives. And there are physical freedoms I miss. Boating. Walking. I love to row. To walk. I walk miles."

"The rowing in the Arno is extremely difficult, alas. But tomorrow, Miss Woolson, we shall walk. Together."

We had strolled through the formal lower reaches of the Boboli Gardens behind the Pitti Palace. The silly statue of Abbondanza was long behind us, and Harry was eyeing a stone bench with something approaching desire. But I had heard of the beautiful view to be had at the summit and was determined to reach it. I hitched my infernal skirt in my hand and climbed. The evening before, I had suffered one of my spells, but had concealed the attack from Clara and Clare so they wouldn't interfere with my plans. The long night had left a muffled, cottony feeling in my ears—and so I didn't hear Harry's wheezing until I reached the top and turned to him, triumphant to have completed the climb. He was several paces behind me, gasping.

The city sat before us in her glory—the glowing red roofs, the Duomo like a divine egg.

He pretended to cough, while struggling to catch his breath.

"I wish this is what I saw every morning at dawn, when I rise to write," I said. "How inspiring." I twisted a bit from my waist and circled each ankle round as we used to in Miss Guilford's comportment classes. If he could pant like a horse, why shouldn't I feel free to stretch my limbs?

"I prefer to work when the sun is high," he said, choking still, trying not to look at my ankles. "What is so urgent that you must rise so early?"

"A few Florentine sketches for *Harper's*. They want them quickly, and they pay so handsomely."

An unhappy frown pinched his brow.

"Mr. James, have I offended you?"

"Not at all, dear Miss Woolson. It's just that they don't pay me anything I'd call handsome." The mention of money seemed to aggravate his wheezing. I resisted the urge to pat his back, as I would do with a small boy.

"I have a more urgent writing challenge than the sketches, I confess, Mr. James. I must resolve the outcome of a novel that *Harper's* has begun to serialize. It is the story of a woman named Anne—a North Lake creature, bold and fierce—who suffers greatly as she makes her way in the world of society. She must even clear the name of the man she loves, who is accused of a heinous crime. I confess I think I love her a little too well, as I see life anew with her young eyes."

He blinked. I continued, excited to have his attention on the subject of my writing, at last. "It's strange how being here has brought the world of my childhood summers to life—the old French trappers and Indians and American soldiers—as if Europe has awakened my imagination. Some days, my memories seem sharper than the streets on which I walk."

"Ah, yes," he said, leaning on a tree. "My lady novelist friend. With your penchant for Negroes, half-breeds, lake maidens, mad confederates, and tradesmen. They've made you very popular, Miss Woolson. And well paid, no doubt. But I am more interested in the interior life, the life of the mind and the emotions."

"But Mr. James," I protested, "surely you, of all people, understand that the interior life is shaped by the world around us. Look at your own heroines. Daisy Miller dreams and suffers in a world not of her making."

"Hidden feelings matter as much in life as public actions do. Often more." His voice quavered and pink blotches began to dot the pale cheeks. Beneath the vest and the beard I saw him tremble. "Relationships are not always what they seem," he insisted. "Or what we want them to be."

"Absolutely!" I agreed. " But as writers don't we try to reveal the truth—what lies beneath? And what actions are then possible, or not, in this tangled world of ours?"

He was silent. I was alarmed by his distress. We had argued amiably about everything from who served the best panna cotta in Florence to the novels of Charles Dickens (which I admired), but here was a point on which I had always imagined we would agree. And everything, at that moment, depended upon it.

"Consider this example, in confidence, Mr. James: it enrages me that I need to rely on my nephew Sam Mather to manage my finances. Sometimes I lie awake at night, tossing with frustration. But it would only do me great harm—curtail my freedom even further—to let those emotions be known to the men in my family! So I behave accordingly. I treat him with exaggerated affection rather than the irritation he deserves."

His grey eyes widened, as if he were seeing me without a bow and arrow for the first time. "Disclosure would lead to censure," he said, slowly. "Less freedom."

"Yes, that is the dilemma of modern female life. The freedom to think, to desire, but not the freedom to act."

"Ah. What you describe is not just a female predicament, I assure you. It is the very tension that inspires me to chronicle, to observe, in my own modest fashion, the human situation."

"And in life, too, surely, Mr. James—you yourself must have experienced this conundrum. You must have felt the world sticking out its foot, to block the path of your own desires."

He gazed out at the vista that lay before us, as if there were a message written for him on the red rooftops. "I have never known anyone to speak in this way, Miss Woolson. You describe what sits in a chest hidden in the attic as clearly as if it were an apple sitting on a table bathed in sunlight."

"Somehow I trust you to let me speak my mind. Your sympathy is a gift, Mr. James. A providential one."

A group of Americans passed by, including a gentleman who had sought my company after a luncheon party weeks earlier. Instinctively, I turned away from their laughter.

When they were gone, Harry touched my arm, ever so slightly, to draw me back to him. I smiled.

"Well, then," he murmured. He breathed deep and slowly, as if he had steadied himself. "I thank you for the honor of your trust. I will do everything I can to deserve it and to provide the same for you. *Siamo simpatici.*"

"*D'accordo. Simpatici*," I smiled.

He bowed, and with a flush, extended his arm. "Shall we?"

Together we made our way down the steep incline. I had to go slowly, to keep in step with him. How I longed to run, run, run down that hill, past the tightly swaying cypresses and the chipped stone benches and the laughing statues.

As he walked me to the pensione, we continued to talk, our words spilling forth on the subjects of writing, and family, and the strain of society, and art . . . When he left my door, my thoughts were racing even faster than my legs had wanted to run. To converse in society demands little of the heart or the mind. And the body can be easily satisfied. But true communication is a stimulant more potent than brandy.

What thrilled me so about him? Evoking feeling has never been my strong suit—as a writer, I am a competent observer of scene and custom, a plodding crafter of story and character, blessed only with the occasional flash of insight that allows me to tell a fleeting truth about the myriad ways—not all romantic—we break each other's hearts. So I strain with every stroke of my pen to explain the deep connection that he and I lit with one another. I could have found him, exhausted our introductions, and moved on. Certainly others have known me as well, or more intimately. But even now, I smile to recall the unequaled joy of never running out of things to say. Only sleep stopped us.

What some discover in youth, I found in middle age. In the sky of that friendship, I flew high. I was the Constance I most wanted to be. Which meant that when one of us hit the ground . . .

Yet, I would give anything to experience that exhilaration again. A marriage not of body, but of minds. I miss it more than anything I have ever known.

Weeks later, when I was packing up to leave Florence, my heart hurt. Clara and Clare had seen their fill of paintings, and Switzerland was the summer destination we had agreed upon. I would have been happy to stay and bask in the warmth of the Tuscan sun. Instead, I vowed to return. Alone.

But I left Florence as a different woman. It had been the place where everything changed. Here my mind had been braided into a plait with someone else's.

It's true that I had sought him out. But after those early weeks together, he could not leave me alone.

Even when miles separated us, he was my constant correspondent. Alice would say that I was the "opium of approval" that poor brother Harry needed to live. But that came later.

CHAPTER THREE

La Vita Romana

*S*oon began the golden days. *Anne* did well—better, the *Harper's* people told me, than any novel serialized in the history of the magazine. (Astoundingly, they actually volunteered to improve on the original contract—doubling my fee and offering to pay royalties on its sales in book form—unheard of for a publisher!) Emboldened by the monies I had earned, I persuaded Clara and Clare that it was time to leave me. At the end of our Grand Tour, the Alpine village of Murren would be our last shared glory.

My strong legs itching for activity, I walked the three-hour Alpine ascent, and Clara followed by

horseback. When she insisted on descending by foot
with me the next day, the effort left her so lame
that she at last cried out for the comforts of home. I
rubbed her blistered little feet in a bath and reminded
her there was no shame in wanting to return to her
family and her life. Truth was, I needed to get on
with mine.

Clara, sweet Clara, wept. I did not.

My eyes were set on Rome. Glorious, golden
Rome. Venice had enthralled me but was too delicious, too stimulating for my first solitary apartment.
Florence was too small, and filled with Americans. I
wasn't seasoned enough to establish my own routine
there. But in Rome, I could be lost. That is where I
decided to make my real start.

Harry's letters kept coming, sometimes two a day.
Playfully, he sought out a pet name for me, trying out
"*La Literatrice*," and "*La Costanza*," until he finally lit
upon my middle name and its echo of my great-uncle,
"Fenimore." I confess I couldn't always keep up with
the pace of his correspondence, given the demands of
my own writing schedule, but I did my best. We shared
not only accounts of our days but story ideas, snippets
of scenes, artistic doubts, and theories. My dream of
an artistic friendship was becoming a reality.

He was agitated by my tales of women artists thwarted by men—especially with a copy of one I sent him in manuscript, called "In the Chateau of Corinne." I tried to explain to him why Geneva's stark beauty and the chateau of the famous French writer Mme. de Staël had moved me so intensely—inspiring me to write the story of an American "Corinne"—a woman poet who is drawn to an arrogant suitor who disdains her genius. When my character Sylvia finally capitulates to her man, I saw the union as the death of her artistic ambitions. Henry, on the other hand, argued that my heroine *wanted* to be "owned" by her husband, that her conquest was a welcome one. Finally I dashed off a short note that said, "My dearest Mr. James, genius though you are, you cannot control the outcome of this lady scribbler's stories!" The response was a beautiful volume of Mme. de Staël's letters, which made me smile every time I looked at it. It still sits on my shelf of favorite volumes, next to so many others sent by Harry over the years.

Yet now I see that his willful dislike of the literary ladies made me doubt myself. I didn't publish that story for years, though *Harper's* accepted it right off, in 1880. It was a long time before I knew to trust the ending—to the dismay of my editor, who was always hungry for another Woolson to fill his pages.

At the time, however, I cherished our communion, and was hungry for the criticisms of the master.
Nearly a year had passed since our Florentine walks,
and we had carved out our own little world apart. I
was separate from his busy society life. He displayed
little interest in my circle of correspondents, friends
like John Hay and Clarence Stedman, nor in my modest social excursions—the teas and suppers for which
I made little time, and even then only for propriety's
sake; nor did he ever have any inkling of the men who
occasionally wandered in and out of my bed. Or, at
least he never let on that he did.

He had shared with me pages of his new book,
The Portrait of a Lady, which promised to be magnificent. At last, I received a letter saying he needed to
see me. The high life of Venice, where he had been
finishing the novel, was taking its toll.

The day we had set for his visit, I sat impatiently
on my small roof garden, surrounded by plants and
terracotta pots and bits of stone statuary. The late April
sun warmed me like a cat, and the Roman palms surrounding the house rustled in the breeze, just as they
had in Florida. The dank smell of old stone and old
life melded with the perfume of the rosemary and
thyme that could have been growing in pots on the

roof for centuries. I closed my eyes and breathed in the perfection of the moment. But I did not want to risk falling asleep, Italian style. I stood up and rested my elbows on the ledge, in a most unladylike fashion. Soon the happy sight of a tall bearded figure in a pale grey suit, clearly not Italian, appeared at the corner. He strolled down the street, taking in the passersby and the buildings as if he had never seen a Roman neighborhood before. I waved but he didn't see me. I knew the Signora would show him in, as I'd told her I was expecting a guest. I scurried down the steps to my main room.

Many minutes later there was a knock at the door. I opened it and bowed.

"Welcome to my sky-parlor!"

He removed his hat, bowed, and extended his hand. "My dear Miss Woolson."

"Please don't stand on such formality, Harry," I said, slapping his hand and giving him a big Cleveland hug around the neck.

He returned the embrace with a good solid squeeze. When I stepped back to look at him he was smiling. "How lovely to see you, *Costanza mia*. Your letters are so full of life, I forgot how the sight of you cheers me." He breathed deep. "But those stairs could be rather more accessible if you're going to entertain lazy guests like myself." He glanced about at the clutch of furniture, the odd stuffed chairs and tables and books and framed pictures that filled my rooms.

"I know these are modest quarters, Harry, by the standards of the ladies and gentlemen with whom you spend so many of your social hours. But I'm just a solitary pioneer, shunning society. All I need are the things I love and a table to write on."

"Well, you have surrounded yourself with so many things, Fenimore, that one can only surmise you possess an extremely promiscuous heart." He closed his left eye in some New England approximation of a wink.

"Ah, it's all the flotsam of a traveling woman's life. I've become the slave of my own trifles. Without a permanent home of my own, all of this takes on too much significance. I can't decide what to keep and what to part with. For example these—Uncle Fenimore's seven Italian prints—if I only kept one or two, would it disrupt the integrity of the set? Or here—his first book contract, with G. P. Putnam's—this is something I cherish."

"There's a strange tribute to a writer—his contract."

"It marks a great moment in his life, when he was able to earn his livelihood by his pen. It inspires me."

"Will you also be framing the statements of your account with *Harper's*, my highly remunerated friend?"

Ah. So it had been a mistake to share with him my glee in my small monetary success. My face burned hot. "Of course not. And popularity does not make me an original such as you, Harry. My work doesn't touch the hem of yours. That much I know."

"My dear Fenimore, I would be very happy to have even a drop of your financial success. If only I could unlock the secrets of you women novelists. Why then—" He stopped.

Nothing annoys a man more than a woman's success at something he wants to do himself. I was sorry I had upset him so early in our visit.

"So, Harry, sit here by the table and tell me about the rich women who are trying to seduce you in Venice."

While I lit the spirit lamp to boil water for our tea, he regaled me with stories of Mrs. Katherine de Kay Bronson's dinner parties, where even Robert Browning was ground into dullness by the hostess's aggressive display of warmth, generosity, and gossip. It seemed that Mrs. Bronson went to great lengths to present herself in flattering light, wearing high collars and surrounding her face with ringlets to give the appearance of youth. I presented an array of pastries on a small painted tray. Harry put one on a plate, considered it carefully, and bit into it with a determined frown, as if he were deciding whether or not to eat a hundred more.

"A woman would tell you that Mrs. Bronson is trying to impress one of the men at her table. The question is, which one? Is it you, Harry? Or Mr. Browning?"

He ignored my question. "Of course there is nothing like sitting on Katherine's balcony with a cigarette and a brandy, watching the rascal gondoliers go by . . . with the right company it is ineffable bliss."

"I too adore Venice."

"But it seems that my artistic and social adventures may be interrupted by a trip back to Boston. Mother hasn't been well. And my sister Alice—dear, ill, beautiful Alice—has relapsed since her visit to England last year. Her neurasthenia strikes hardest in moments of emotional stress, making her condition an added worry to us all, I'm afraid. However, I have no longing to return to the tight little sphere of Boston society. I can tell you, Fenimore, that I would much prefer to burrow into my London flat after this Venetian spell."

"Ah, your little world of Nortons and Lowells and

Holmeses and Adamses. How exotic it is to me, really, with my Western wildness," I answered.

"I can assure you, the combination of Boston society and my father's presence has never been an aid to creativity—or digestion."

The whistle of the kettle interrupted him. I silenced the sputtering pot and brought the brewing tea to the table where the plate of cakes was now half empty. As I busied myself pouring, straining, sugaring the cups, he was quiet, or so I thought. I looked up at him to hand him his cup.

"Well, do you?" he asked, agitated.

"Do I what?"

"I just asked if you think I am capable of creating a girl who readers will believe in."

"Forgive me, Harry. My bad ear doesn't always catch every word."

Abruptly he placed his cup on the table. "I am losing faith in myself and my heroine Isabel. The older woman, Mme. Merle—the jaded one who is orchestrating the liaison between my heroine and this woman's former lover—is taking over the tale."

"Oh, Harry, no. What I have read so far is brilliant. Your *Portrait of a Lady* is going to be the best thing you've ever written, I assure you."

He said nothing, twirling the cake plate with his thumb.

"Poor Isabel—poor idealizing American girl. How well you know her, Harry. But remember to let us see whether or not Isabel really loves her husband. Even though we can see that he betrays her, we need to know whether she loved just the European idea of him, or the man himself. That determines what she goes through—agony or acceptance—afterward. And how much we should hurt on her behalf."

"I prefer to leave such interpretations to the imagination of the reader."

"But she is your creation, Harry. What heart have you given her?" I paused. "I fear that I love my heroines too much. You could stand for a bit of that, you know—it is one of those secrets of the lady novelists. Allow yourself to fall in love with your heroine, and you will see her as your readers do."

He sipped his tea and returned the cup to the small table. "But I don't want to be hampered by what you call love. I would rather risk everyone's wrath, and explore the true agonies of life. Readers, especially lady readers, think only of the happy outcome for a character they have learned to love."

"If you don't give her happiness, you have to give her insight, understanding, some inner rather than outer change."

"That's it, exactly, *Costanza mia!* The inner change." He patted his knees with excitement. "Truth is, I have been hatching a plan for several novels. Explorations of the theme we spoke of that warm day in the Boboli Gardens—the mystery of what we can ever know about any human heart. The drama of discovery, rather than the false drama of action."

His enthusiasm was palpable—I was staring at his lips, reading them, so that I wouldn't lose any of the words that poured out of him.

"How do you do that, Harry? How do you dramatize a realization? A change of heart?"

"Our friendship has helped me to see that women are the best vehicle for this effort—pulled as they are between society and the interior life."

"Why, Harry," I clapped my hands. "Why don't you think of it this way—you are reinventing what you have always dismissed as the overused women's plots—courtship, marriage, betrayal. Now they will take on a new, modern meaning. Women changing, thinking, taking charge of their own lives."

"Or learning to live with the heartache of what cannot be."

Of course, my wildly successful *Anne*, like so many first novels, had suffered from a surfeit of plot—what Harry would call the false drama of action. And my heroine possessed such a driven and restless nature that some might say she couldn't sit still—she had done everything from being a teacher to a Civil War nurse to a singer in a choir to a detective. But then again, she had to earn her living. It is women of means who can afford to sit and live with heartache, I would have said to my brilliant friend if I had been bolder, or wiser. Instead, I was dazzled to be in his confidence.

"What an extraordinary undertaking, Harry. It is magnificent." I touched his hand. "No wonder you joke so about wanting to know the secrets of the lady novelists. Perhaps someday you'll even create a woman who interests us for reasons other than romance—say, a lady artist with ambition? Or the deep relationship between two women—friends, sisters, rivals? There are so many untold stories of what goes on in a woman's heart and mind. Only George Eliot has ever begun to explore them."

"Two women? I'm not sure that even Madame Eliot could plumb the strange private world that my

sister Alice and her companion Katherine inhabit
. . . But your encouragement means everything to
me, *Costanza*. There isn't another soul with whom
I could discuss my work before the pen is set to
paper." Suddenly, he seemed embarrassed. "So, show
me this famous roof garden you've written about so
eloquently."

He followed me up the iron steps to my bower
in the sky. He took in my little chair and table, the
plants, the pots, the terracotta tiles.

"What a funny solitary bird you are, Fenimore. I
imagine you nesting up here by yourself, surrounding
yourself with straw and feathers and small treasures.
But don't you miss company?"

"There are always invitations, Harry. Every now
and then some English or American family realizes
who I am, and asks me to dinner. Horrid. I accept as
few of the offers as possible."

He saw the copy of Epictetus open on the table
and picked it up. "The Stoics are strong stuff for a
woman alone, aren't they?"

"Not for this one, Harry. 'Make trial of your
power and you will know how far it reaches.'"

Two men—one middle aged and thick but ele-
gantly dressed, one slender and nymph-like, handsome

but not as smartly clad—stopped in the street below us. With agitation, they argued, the older man becoming more upset with each flail of his arm.

"Do you remember our game in the Piazza that day in Florence, *Costanza*? What do you make of these two? Arguing over a young heiress of whom they are both enamored?"

I peered over the ledge and pretended to give the two men careful scrutiny. "Not at all, dear Harry. This older man is in love with the younger man and is begging him not to run off for a month in Capri with the Duke of Mantua, who, of course, doesn't deserve him and despite his title doesn't have the means of our portly friend here."

He gasped and turned his back to the street. "That is rather sordid, Fenimore."

"Oh, Harry, don't be such a Bostonian. Remember that we're in Europe now. Besides, no one should be judged for the object of his affection. As Epictetus wisely points out, 'Is freedom anything else other than the right to live as we wish? Nothing else.'"

"Is that what Epictetus says? Then I shall have to take him up." He smiled and glanced at the men in the street, who were now walking arm in arm. "I'm afraid I have an engagement this evening, Fenimore, then back to Venice tomorrow."

"I am honored as always to have a fragment of your time, master."

"*Costanza*, it is primarily to see you that I came to Rome. Would you care to accompany me tonight to the home of Mrs. Van Rensselaer?"

"Don't speak of it, Harry. I want to savor our afternoon rather than struggle to get through the tedium of a dinner. Besides, *La Rensellina* needs to have you all to herself."

"I thank you, then, for this most exquisite afternoon. Promise me you'll make your way to London after this Italian sojourn? Once I'm back from my Boston visit you must join me in England. You would love the literary life of London. And we would be near each other."

"It's a lovely plan. We'll correspond about it, along with many other matters, grand and small." I looked up at his large, beautiful face. "Be proud, Harry. A man writing a portrait of a lady—imagine a woman writing a portrait of a gentleman! We women can only know what men do and say—what they think nobody but a ghost could know."

"And you, Fenimore—keep up those short stories. They seem quite your metier, those compact narratives of intense little women artists and their thwarted ambitions to work in the realm of men." He held my hand and kissed it. Then he made off down the stairs.

Of course the *Portrait* was his first true masterpiece. He was already finished with it, really, when he came to ask for reassurance about it. We never do find out whether or not Isabel loved her cynical husband—it is the great gap at the center of an otherwise brilliant book. But no one else seemed to mind. The critics adored it, lauding it as an extraordinary realization of the mind of a young modern woman. I agreed with them all. It took me years to realize how hard it had been for Harry to send his own character back to that awful husband.

It always bothered Harry that he didn't sell as many copies of *Portrait* as I had of *Anne*, which was far the lesser book.

There was another thing I didn't quite understand that lovely day in Rome. Whenever Harry left he always took something from me, a little piece of my own imagination. The danger of sharing, perhaps? My heart, I was willing to give. But not my stories. Or my ambition to work in the world of men.

I answered him, as I would so many times, in the form of a story. I wrote "In the Street of the Hyacinth," the tale of a female American painter, an innovator, whose gift is destroyed by the criticisms of the mentor she seeks out in Rome. I had quite a bit of fun with this story, creating a younger version of myself—a western lass who boldly demands time and attention from the established critic Raymond Noel, in quest of whom she has come all the way to Rome. In my story, Ettie finally succumbs to the man who destroyed her artistic dreams, and agrees to marry him (having turned down a painter and an Italian count!) . . . not because I wanted to marry anyone (including Harry), but because I had not yet figured out how to tell a tale without relying on the "false drama of action."

Besides, I knew such a plot would drive him crazy.

CHAPTER FOUR

The Year of Vesuvius

*A*mericans, like Harry, leave Rome too early. Just when the city comes alive—as the overcoats are tossed aside, as the stones of the churches lose their chill, as the fountains' cold drizzle turns to the welcome spray of relief—they go north. So I stayed to continue my Roman experiment, savoring my solitude and the ease of life in my sky parlor, writing stories and sketches for *Harper's*.

Save for the occasional note, Harry went silent for several months after his visit. He claimed that Venetian society, the journey back to London, were making too great demands on him. In fact, he had told me too much. This I understood better than he did. One of the reasons I guard my time so jealously is that I fear conversation—whatever answer I give to the inevitable question, "And what are you working on now?" will dissipate the urge to tell my stories on the page.

When the heat came hard, like an oven, I retreated to my beloved Alps. But the south sang to me. So, in the autumn of that wandering year I returned not to Rome but further even than Naples, to Sorrento. How I adored the Amalfi coast. Cliffs as high as at Mackinac Island but white white against a sea bluer than any I'd ever seen in Florida. And there were orange and lemon groves everywhere. Heaven.

Is there anything more luxurious than selling descriptions of pink villas and terraces and the gorgeous Bay of Naples to a magazine? I think not. To *Harper's*, and on occasion *Atlantic Monthly*, I owed then, and now, much of my happiness and independence. Of course my niece and nephew and assorted other friends and relations were alarmed by my solitary journey to the land of Pompeii. You'd think that Vesuvius was going to erupt on my head and freeze me there for eternity. Which would have been fine with me—to become a small relic for all eternity, near the scent of lemon and in sight of the blue sea. I would have walked to the volcano's edge if I could be assured of such an end for myself. Instead, I settled for long walks in the hills surrounding my villa and the sight of the smoke smoldering from Vesuvius's mouth.

Harry had returned home to the States, as he expected. While he was there his mother died, which shook him to the core. It was difficult to tell what shocked him more: the loss, or the force with which the loss hit him. He was like a man who is hit by a train, who keeps talking about the train being two minutes earlier than scheduled instead of his severed limb. The letters began to come in a rush, filled with sorrow and need. Harry became strangely impatient with my wanderings, as if he needed to think of me fixed in one spot that he could choose to visit or not. Though my mail was always forwarded by my bank in Germany, he became afraid that he would lose track of me. I did my best to calm him, to remind him of our times together. He was homesick for Europe as much as my winning self. But the truth is I had other things on my mind.

I was hungry, ravenous to see and live as much as possible. The pain in my ear had abated, and whenever I had a respite from the force of the clenching fist in my head, I seized my opportunity. The road was open to me.

In addition to my travel sketches, I had decided to write a new novel—not a tale of a thwarted woman artist, or of a young girl making her way, but of an older woman and what she was prepared to do for the love of a man. Inspired by Henry's comment about Mrs. Bronson, I invented a middle-aged woman who devoted her life to deceiving her second husband about her age—even denying the existence of the adult son of her first marriage. She wore high collars, old-fashioned curls, kept her lights low. Everything she did, she did "For the Major." This became the title of my novella when it was serialized the following year, in 1883.

It would have been easy to set my tale amidst the tight society of Americans abroad. But the hills of the American South, and the gossipy, close-knit cliques of small-town life, filled my imagination. So, immersed in my tale, I re-created the villages of North Carolina that Mother and I had once explored. The southern voices came to life in my mind with more clarity than the muffled drone of the Europeans and Americans around me in Italy. As summer waned I left the coast and made my way to Florence, but the American scene there was a tedious distraction. Unlike Harry, I did not find dinner parties conducive to creative work. And all I could hear was the voice of Mrs. Carroll, my heroine. I identified with her urge to pin up her grey hair and wash the paint off her face. What freedom she must have felt in old age.

It was a solitary life, living with the company of my characters. So when my old friend John Hay invited me to join his family and friends for an autumn sojourn in Paris, I could not resist. This wonderful, remarkable man, once secretary to President Lincoln, was one of my old Ohio connections, married to the sister of my nephew Sam's wife (though it must be said that Clara Hay never seemed a soulmate for her sensitive husband). While Clara shopped at Worth, John was spending his Parisian days in search of relief from the despair that we often discussed in our letters—the recurrent demons that threaten to strangle one before coffee in the morning. John even sought help from the renowned Dr. Jean Charcot, but when Europe's leading neurologist could only advise him to "buck up," John bravely tried to do just that.

Here was a man who didn't wait for a gaggle of stray Americans of a certain income level to waddle into town for inane receptions and dinners. Instead, he assembled the group he wanted for several weeks of theater, opera, and conviviality. He had booked rooms for several of us at the Grand Hotel. While I was there, he wrote, he wanted to introduce me to the only man he could imagine sparking my interest in marriage. He was right about the man, though not about marriage.

There is a kind of woman who insists on loving a man who lacks all the qualities universally considered agreeable in a gentleman. Among my sex, I am that kind of woman. And so my little boat was capsized by Clarence King. An explorer, a geologist, a man of science—King was a rough-hewn self-invention whose company was regularly sought out by the less adventurous husbands and sons who felt braver in his reflected light. Women of society did not understand him—he made no pretense of interest in the latest hair fashion or the flirtation witnessed at last night's dance. The instant I laid eyes on his square face, his thick-shouldered frame, I felt a hot rush of attraction to him. It was an irrational pull, coming from my most unconscious self. Harry was a passion of the mind; King was, quite simply, a passion.

It was rumored that King had a Negro mistress back home, and a brood of mulatto children. I never asked, and I never cared. It is true that he was the only American I ever met in Europe who spoke of black people as if they were fellow members of the human race. For this alone I might have loved him. But King also took me to late-night clubs where women danced with each other and where men wore skirts. He taught me how to order wines and how to drink them. He discussed medicine and the new theories of the mind with me. He loved my stories of the lakes and the South, and urged me to set a longer novel in my beloved Florida. Someday soon, he said, the world will be ready for real American writing, stories that explore the pressures of race and class and self-invention, not just superficial tales that shadow European social mores. Melville, poor reviled Melville, would have his day. And the world would embrace its women artists, like me.

King, how you gave me courage.

King was the most purely American creation, more devoted to personal freedom than any creature I had ever encountered. "If we can create our country, why not our selves?" he asked. Though he was not a philosopher, he was a stoic without realizing it. "We are what we do, how we act," he liked to say. The antithesis of Harry, who insisted always that we are not what we do, but what we feel. In Harry's world, it seems, we are defined exactly by what we don't do!

One night when King and I were alone in my rooms, I was seized by a fierce spasm of pain on the left side of my head. I tried to rise from the bed but was too dizzy to walk. Embarrassed, I hid my face in the sheet and tried to steady the awful hammer with slow breathing, as I often did when alone. King arranged the pillows beneath me, stroked my head, sang to me to soothe me. Then he made me confess to him what was wrong.

"I am prone to spells of sadness, just like my father," I explained. "But this is not a sinking of spirit, of will." The tears mounted, despite my efforts to stay calm. "I have these seizures of pain in my head, especially behind the left ear. My hearing is already diminished."

"Connie, you need the attention of a first-rate physician."

"Whenever a woman is ill, doctors accuse her of being a hysteric. Or a neurasthenic. Or a melancholic. It is insulting." I surrendered to sobs, finally. He held me and I felt the silk of his robe. Even through my pain I savored the scent of pipe and soap.

"You must see one of the new doctors. England or Germany is the place."

"My German isn't good enough to speak to a doctor in German."

"Then, England. I know just the man."

"King, you are a good man. Even in these unconventional circumstances." I pulled the bedclothes over my nightdress. "Like my character, Mrs. Carroll, I am too old for romance. I should hide such infirmities from you. You must find me to be far more work than you bargained for."

"I bargained for nothing but the chance to know a remarkable woman." He kissed my forehead, gently.

The next morning I rose for breakfast much stronger. King had given me not just affection, but hope. Sitting in the hotel dining room, glancing at the newspaper like a businessman in a train station while I sipped my café au lait, I was joined by John Hay and Henry Adams. Though Hay had an apartment with his wife and three children, he liked to join his "visitors" for breakfast whenever possible.

"You're looking well, Connie," cooed Hay. "Perhaps Cupid's arrow has struck at last—pierced the heart of the goddess to whom mere mortal men are just a vain show?"

"Whatever do you mean, John?" I asked, tearing off a piece of croissant.

"Since you arrived, you seem to relish the company of Clarence King, and no one else."

I smiled at him, knowing that the truth would be beyond his wildest imaginings. "You've hit it on the nose, John. I absolutely adore Clarence King. I can think of no one else."

"Magnificent!" chortled Adams. "Wait until Harry gets here. Won't he be jealous."

"Harry?" I asked, startled.

"Harry James—he is back on this side of the Atlantic."

"Yes, that I know. So he wrote to me."

"Well, don't you think he should spend his rainy October days here in Paris with us, rather than touring around those wet Loire towns with Fanny Kemble and her weary party?" asked John.

"When is he due to arrive?"

"As soon as tomorrow, I hope. We have tickets for the Opera for this Friday."

"Alas, I'm afraid I shall miss him," I said. "I am expected in Florence and will be setting off tomorrow afternoon."

"Connie! How dreadful. Why not change your plans?"

"I'm afraid that's not possible." I folded my napkin. "And now, if you'll excuse me, I have to spend my final hours with the beloved Mr. King, who is everything to me."

With a small bow, I left them, mouths agape.

King and I had a farewell lunch that day. I searched for the words to explain why I could not carry on with him in front of Harry. But of course, I did not understand the reason very well myself. All it came down to was that I knew, in my soul, that it would upset Harry. Possessive, selfish, egotistical Harry—who did not want to woo me or any woman—would be distressed.

"I just won't feel free, that is, to be as we have been, with Henry James here," I tried to explain. "It sounds foolish, I know. But his friendship matters greatly to me. And he is so ruled by propriety."

"You think James is ruled by propriety?" Clarence smiled.

"Why, yes. It is everything to him. I fear he already finds me a bit of a wild frontier creature."

"James lives with the voice of a disapproving father figure in his ear, it's true. Someday the new science of the mind will help those like him to dethrone that voice. But having seen James in the company of men, I don't think he is as squeamish as you do. He's a bit of a roué, a dandy."

"That may be. Still, I am loath to jeopardize the bond we've established, he and I. It sounds absurd, King. But I also want to protect what we've had—I don't want our freedom together compromised by his presence."

"Connie, there's no need to explain. I'm not a man who requires explanations. I shall never do anything to interfere with the good feelings between you and Harry James. Though I dare say, that he doesn't understand you a bit. He never will." He took my hand and held it tight. "My frontier woman. Write a wonderful novel set in the South for me, will you?"

I nodded.

"And this is not good-bye for us. We shall share other adventures. But before we meet again, you must see one of the doctors I recommend. You are determined to begin with Dr. Baldwin, in Florence?"

"Yes, I am. He is already well spoken of, and I know Florence well. If he sends me to London, then that will be my next stop."

"Excellent. So, where should we go for our last night together in Paris? It is your choice, Connie."

"I know exactly what I want to do tonight."

We did not leave my rooms that evening. The next morning, I rose at dawn and took my café in my room. King arranged for a driver to take me to the Gare d'Orleans, since I insisted on going alone. From the window of my train compartment, I watched the curtain of water fall in sheets over the grey Paris suburbs. I was running away from Harry. And because of him I was leaving King behind, not knowing when or if I'd ever see him again. Suddenly, the friendship I had sought out with Harry felt like a yoke to me. I was surprised by the vehemence with which I wanted to shake it off.

CHAPTER FIVE

Ring Around the Rosy

And so two new men entered my life: King and Dr. William Wilberforce Baldwin. Dr. Baldwin is so well known now that it's difficult to remember how young and untried he seemed the first time he greeted me in his visiting room, when he had just arrived in Florence. He became my doctor, my advisor, my friend. And for the next ten years he did his best to stop the hammer in my head. Later, of course, I introduced him to the Jameses. He was a godsend not just to Harry but also, more urgently, to Alice.

There was very little I did not end up sharing with the acquisitive, voracious Jameses. Only King. And, once I had learned my lesson, a few plain truths.

After I left Paris, Harry did not stay long to ca-
vort with his chums. By early December Alice telegrammed to say that their father was dying. It turned
out that Henry Senior had decided he did not want to
live without his sainted, devoted wife, that paragon of
female subservience. And so he had spent the better
part of the year starving himself to death. It was the
final rebuke to his children. Poor Harry's ship docked
the day the funeral took place.

Florence in the meantime was a most vexing
winter pleasure. The demands of Florentine expatri-
ate society were invented for people who have too
much time on their hands and are looking for ways
to fill it. How could I work all morning and then take
my regular walks and gallery visits, when my precious
afternoons were supposed to be devoted to receptions
and paying calls? Every time someone left a card for
me, I was required to repay the visit on that family's
visiting day, and that day only. I tried to explain my
frustration to William Dean Howells, who was visiting
for two months with his wife. He laughed and said I
was taking work much too seriously. I should take a
page from Harry and enjoy myself. But Harry did not
live with the ringing in his ears, that hinted of mortality far louder than time's winged chariot.

That April a letter was forwarded to me in Venice, where I had gone to escape the pressures of Florence—and to meet King. The streaked and blotted handwriting led me to suspect the writer was intoxicated when he penned it:

My dear Fenimore:

You warned me, with your usual wisdom, how strange it is to find oneself without any parents, even in the prime of one's own middle years. Father's death has left an ache that I could not have anticipated—a hole in the heart. I spent the first three days in Cambridge sleeping, sleeping, like a fairy princess who had swallowed a potion—in my father's bed. When I awoke, I knew I was truly alone.

Free, my brother William might say.

Did I ever make my father happy? To be raised by an unconventional parent of strong spirit is like coming of age in a fancy racing boat whose captain doesn't know something as simple as how to dock in a harbor. Father so wanted each of us boys to be spectacular—nothing mundane, such as a school prize or a sporting ribbon, would do. For this purpose he tore us, with Mother and Aunt Kate and Alice, all over Europe, back to Newport and then to Europe again. . . . My younger brothers Wilky and Bob each set off to make their fortunes in the conventional manner, though neither succeeded. For what did William and I avoid service in the War, if not to fulfill our father's great ambitions for us? We were to rise to the magnificence, the rare imagination, the character, that he wanted for us—without ever fighting him or deploring him in the details.

I have never confessed to anyone that I have always suspected Father saw my paltry writings as girls' work—the business of lady scribblers (apologies, Litteratrice Mia, *but I speak not of course of the higher variety such as yourself but the Fanny Ferns and Maria Cumminses of our childhood). William has always had the more scientific, the more curious, the more paternally satisfying, genius.*

So now, at least, I can never disappoint my father again, in my writing or my life. But the ache, Fenimore, the ache—

What would give me great solace, Costanza, *would be to take one of our walks today. Our time in Rome saved me, not to mention the* Portrait. *I would be happy to shout for you and you poor little ears in order to enjoy the sympathy of our friendship. Your affectionate trust, your discretion, have calmed me in the face of many distractions and defeats. What a tender friendship we have erected. But more than anything I miss laughing together. If only you were here to observe the social niceties of grief, New England style, I know my spirits would lighten. Your fine humor and power of satiric observation always cast* la comedie humaine *in the proper light.*

I know how much you love Italy, but your friend entreats you to come to London when I return there. The literary scene is very lively and will inspire you. It will fall to me, I expect, to bring my sister Alice and her companion with me to England at some point in the near future. Alice roused herself in father's final months, bravely, but is now lost without the daughterly ministrations to consume her attention. And our Aunt Kate is not the right companion for my strong-willed sister. To put it most bluntly, I think they would drive each other mad. Though of course my own vocation will prevent me from ever keeping house with my sister Alice (or anyone for that matter), I have agreed with William that we should help to set her up in rooms in London, near my own.

Fenimore, abandon the decadent charms that drew you to Paris. (Yes, even here in my provincial New England world I do hear of assignations and romances abroad.) John Hay has your interests at heart but is not as steady an influence as he seems. The truth is that Clarence King is a louche and an adventurer of the worst sort—he is rumored to have a Negro family in Brooklyn!—and he doesn't deserve you. No man does. But this man, your friend Harry, needs you. Even though you should never see the darkest side of his nature, as it were . . .

From your letter it sounds as if you need some cheering yourself. No more morbid allusions to death and the other world.

That ear will be fit in no time—perhaps you should take the waters at Bournemouth?

Forgive these personal effluences from a son's saddened heart. As you know I detest the appearance of a tear-soaked handkerchief on any page, even a personal one.

Lest you think that my duties as executor have left me consumed with black draperies and the inventories of the family manse (though I take with utter seriousness the responsibilities that Father gave to me rather than William, and have been setting right the inequities concerning my brother Wilky) the Portrait *has made me quite a well-known figure here. Of course the royalties don't exceed yours. Now I am contemplating a story set in Boston about a new woman—or the pull between the old and the new. Just as you suggested in Rome. Now there's a subject that father would have abhored.*

Write to me soon, dearest Fenimore,

Your devoted, Harry

I folded the letter and looked up from the enormous carved writing table that filled a corner of my Venetian rooms, which I had found at the top of an old palazzo on the Grand Canal. No one else had been willing to walk the stairs to the top floor, so they had come at a good price.

"Henry James says you're a louche," I said to King, who was standing on the balcony, hands in his pockets, enjoying the glorious view. His packed valise was sitting at my feet.

"Well, he should know." He flashed his terrific, crooked smile at me. "What does he want from you this time?"

"Nothing, really. He's just trying to recover from his father's death. He did beg me to come to London."

"Forsooth! The boldness of the man. I'll challenge the devil to a duel!" mocked King, with his hand over his forehead.

We looked at each other for one solemn moment and burst out laughing. "The truth is, I'm on my way there to consult the ear specialist that Dr. Baldwin wants me to see. So I will most certainly see our mutual friend. John Hay will be able to tell you where to find me—if you are so inclined."

"I'll write to you from the Rockies, Connie, that much is certain. But only if you promise to get cracking on the Florida novel."

"Well, I shall get cracking, as you put it, as soon as you've left me to the peace of my work. That is, after all, why I came to Venice in the first place. But first, you must keep your word, and take that gondola ride with me. A gondola is perfection in motion—and I want to experience perfection with you."

The June sea breeze danced through the window, blowing the drapes and ruffling the papers on my desk and tousling King's unruly hair. I yearned to sail with it through the canals and the piazzas and the windows. He seemed to read my thoughts.

"For you, Connie, I shall sit in one of those damnable boats with the silly fellow with the pole. *Andiamo.*"

So I headed north to London, but not for the reasons Harry thought.

CHAPTER SIX

Waiting for Alice

I could have lived without sound. That is not to say that I didn't love the world's music. More than a single human voice, I would have missed the roar of dry leaves in the autumn wind. The ceaseless ocean waves beating on the shore, in Florida or Positano. Children laughing in the park, running in circles around their nanny. Dogs barking happily in the snow, running home for dinner at twilight. The building chorus of waking birds just before dawn. The exhilarating cacophony of an orchestra tuning up before the start of a performance. Whenever I thought my hearing had left me for good, I would rehearse these sounds in my mind, to preserve them.

But when the pain struck, I feared I would not live, period. My courage fled as soon as the fist tightened in my head, squeezing tight on the right side so that I thought my vessels would burst. When the fist clenched, I could not think, or write. Or remember.

This is why I followed Dr. Baldwin's advice, and traveled to London to submit to the treatment offered by Dr. Aloysius Snow.

I did not like Snow. Unlike Dr. Baldwin, he did not have the gift of listening. This was ironic, given that he specialized in disorders of the ear. But at least he did not strip me bare and poke my abdomen to discern the "hysterical" roots of my problem, as so many doctors had done. Snow was a man of science. Since the problem was in my ears, he focused on what happened above rather than below my waist.

"Someday soon, Miss Woolson," he shouted, accustomed no doubt to patients who were stone deaf, "we'll be able to take a picture of the inside of your head. Medicine is on the verge of a new era." He pressed the back of my neck with his thick fingers. "Let's continue with the poultices and neck massages."

And so through that first English winter I continued with the most foul-smelling soaks ever to be administered by the maid at Sloane Street, where I had taken rooms. Though it was never bitter cold, as in Cleveland or Cooperstown, I was in constant need of a fire. With its fine cold mist, the English air was drowning me as no ocean had ever done. Snow claimed there was no scientific basis in my preference for heat. But the damp could never shock me into health the way my beloved Italy had done. I took solace in the green parks of London where I'd walk in the dim sunlight every afternoon. And of course, with the heated Florida world of my newest novel, *East Angels*, with which I spent every morning. I lost myself in the stew of relations among Spaniards, Floridians, and New England visitors in a down-at-heels Florida town after the war. In Margaret Harold, who refuses to leave the husband who has left her twice, I created a heroine as stoic, as suffering, as my heart could bear. As long as I could walk, and write, and walk, and write, I kept the hammer at bay.

Having begged me to join him in London, Harry made sure I understood how very busy he was as soon as I arrived. He led a very segmented social life—a dinner party here, a salon there, a country house flirtation—to distract and disarm—on the side. The notion that his women friends were competing for his attention was a fantasy that he labored to maintain. It was as if I knew two Harrys—the public acquaintance, who could kill with politesse, and the private friend, who could ignite my spirit with even the smallest spark of true intimacy. But those small sparks were precious.

And so I did not reveal to him, ever, the full extent of my medical battles. Without understanding why, I simply knew that the harsh intrusion of an ugly reality such as illness would repulse him. It would prevent us from being each other's golden mirror, keep us from reflecting only the ideal selves we were yet to become. Nor did I share with Harry the darkness that set in when I received word that my only brother, Charley, had died in San Francisco. No official cause was given, but I suspect morphine and alcohol. Harry's own younger brother Wilky passed shortly after. But he was not ready to speak of yet another family loss.

The truth is that Harry had returned from Boston an older, sadder man—marked by care, but even more by a grim determination to be lauded by the public. One does not have to be a great writer, like Harry, to know that the quest for admiration will doom any artist. But he was as hungry for praise as he was for a fine supper.

One night I encountered the public Harry with the infamous actress Fanny Kemble at the theater where Salvini was performing in *Othello*. Boosted by a good spell with my ears, I had bought myself a ticket to rouse myself from the wintry gloom. Harry was in high form, his cheeks flushed, his manner exaggerated and grand. Kemble led him, wrapped in silk and furs, the diamonds sparkling from her still-lovely ears. As they had the better seats, Harry insisted on giving up his to leave me with the actress. She looked at my simple blue suit, my modest necklace, and purred, "I am so sorry that Mr. James has introduced you to me. I shall not speak to you, or look at you, or be conscious of your existence, even, for the entire evening." I was miserable. For what did he make the gesture? Not to please me, certainly. Not to please her. But out of some misplaced sense of himself as courtier. I had a flash of anger toward him, for so ruining everyone's evening but his own. In that moment he seemed dangerous to me.

As soon as the days lengthened I left London for the countryside. It is in the small villages and towns that England is most herself, most alive. Having always longed to live in a cathedral town, I took rooms in Salisbury—right in the Close itself, in the home of the one of the cathedral vergers. What heaven after the crowds of the city! Long green walks beneath glorious trees, the spire in view no matter how many miles I traversed; buildings dating back to Shakespeare's time, with leaden-framed panes and beams outside; and in the cathedral itself, my own stall right near the organ, so that I could appreciate the music, from a vantage as close as possible, in all its glory. From Salisbury I ventured forth on short trips, to Stratford and Oxford and Kenilworth . . . letting coach or train deliver me to villages that a woman could traverse alone in a day.

In the evenings I read Charley's diary, sent to me by Clara after she'd gone through his box of paltry effects. It was a wrenching encounter, one that I had to wrestle with alone as the late summer light stretched across the green outside my window. To confront his pain, his fear, his hatred of me—was a solitary sorrow.

The selfish truth was, I wasn't sorry that I hadn't known the depth of his despair. It might have held me stateside. But my heart was heavy.

One blowy September morning I walked to Salisbury Plain. Planting my feet firmly against the wind, I faced the ancient shapes of Stonehenge, and asked them to share with me their secrets. Nothing answered me except the wind. I turned slowly to take in the landscape. A tall, heavyish man in a city suit was waving to me, trotting toward me from a carriage that stood behind him. As I stood, holding my shawl beneath my chin, I realized that the man was Henry James.

He neared me, panting, and holding his hat to keep it from blowing away.

"Harry! I thought you were still in Dover."

"The season there is over. And I did write to say that I was coming to visit, *Costanza mia*."

"True enough, Harry. But I didn't expect you until next week." The wind howled. "Come, have you ever really seen the stones up close? They're magnificent." I grabbed his hand and ran for the cover of the ancient altar.

"See, it's quieter here. Perhaps that was part of the original design."

He shivered.

"King says there are even more spectacular stone formations in Mexico and South America. I would love to go there."

"Please, Fenimore. Not the cowboy geologist."

"My brother Charley never visited Europe. But how he wanted to see Stonehenge. He writes of it in the diary he kept, which my sister sent me."

"Do you miss him?"

"I didn't know him. I can't pretend I miss the person. He was always so much the focus of my mother's concern, for all the years I tended to her . . . I suppose I resented him. And now I see that he in turn resented me. But I am left hurting for the possibility of him."

"It is the same with Wilky. My father was so very hard on him. It is the drinkers who steal a piece of our heart, as they are nothing but unexplored potential." His eyes filled with tears. "It is just as windy here, you know, my friend."

"Then let's go back to my lodgings. It's the season for geese and pheasants and partridge. I'm sure there will be something delicious."

The verger set us a lovely table. The wine was better than usual, I noticed.

"I just received a letter saying that my sister Alice will be arriving in two months' time."

"To be with you? How wonderful."

"Not to me. In no sense to me. She is extremely independent. Especially that is, when it comes to her friend, Katherine Loring."

"Harry. Please. No need to elaborate. I believe the term for such companionship is, appropriately enough, a 'Boston marriage'?"

"The truth is, I do not think the dependence on Katherine is healthful, in the long run. Yet, I must accept it with gratitude because without her, well . . . I should have to take Alice completely on my own shoulders. That is impossible, don't you see?"

"I do, Harry. I do." I poured more wine into his glass. "Harry, no apologies needed. The writing must come first. And for the writing to come first, you need your freedom. I understand completely."

"You see, I have signed a new agreement with Osgood for my next two novels—I've disposed of all rights for a princely sum. The first shall be a private history of the new public woman. Mrs. Humphrey Ward did not get it right, I'm afraid. I shall yet do something great, Fenimore."

Alice arrived in the country flat on her back, and spent the better part of a year getting to the sitting position. Though she was never at a loss for visitors, I gave her as much time as I could, first as a favor to Harry, but eventually because I learned to cherish the unique female camaraderie that she and Katherine Loring offered. I was by nature a man's woman, but savored the rapport that Alice offered in her strange salon. She saw the world as no one else did.

This is not to say that the sister did not share her brother's demanding nature, though it was expressed as a demand for attention rather than as a cry for privacy. Whenever Katherine had to leave Alice's side to tend to her own sister, Henry was forced take the companion's place—a role he detested. His relief when they made their nest in London rather than Bournemouth (where the Lorings had been staying) was palpable. That fall, despite the demands of Dr. Snow's treatments and finishing *East Angels*, I was expected to make my weekly visits to Alice's flat.

In December of 1885, we learned that Henry Adams's wife, Clover, had killed herself by ingesting the potassium chloride that she used to develop her wonderful photographs. Clover had been a close friend of Alice's from her Cambridge days. As soon as I read John Hay's telegram, I hurried to Alice's home, expecting to find Harry nursing her through the crisis. But Harry, it turned out, could not bring himself to dwell on anything as distasteful as depression, or even worse, suicide.

"She could not bear the loss of her father," said Alice, after Katherine had removed a cloth from her forehead. "Henry Adams is a cold and peculiar fish. He could never help Clover when the demons grabbed her by the throat."

"I know those dark spirits myself," I said, returning my teacup to the tray. "I inherited them from my own father."

"But surely your writing lessens the hold of despair, Constance?"

"So far, it does. But will it always?" I took her hand, which was much stronger than I expected it to be. "Truth is, Alice, I don't think that it is the worse thing in the world to end one's own suffering. I would rather stop living, without warning, than try to live when courage has failed me."

"That is our stoic philosopher speaking," murmured Katherine.

"Of course, it is harder on those who are left behind than on the one who has departed," I said.

"I love Clover, and I forgive her," wailed Alice. "In fact, I admire the terrible bravery of it, despite the shock. And of course the fact that the secret of her pain is now revealed to all."

"Not secret to those who loved her."

"But secret from the world of prying eyes. My own father once gave me permission to kill myself, as if it were his to give. Ha! As if I would make it so easy for him. Better that he endure my illnesses, my nervous condition."

She grabbed my other hand and pulled me to her with fierce power. "You must understand, Constance. We Jameses are insatiable. We always want more than we are willing to give. That's what comes of growing up hungry."

By winter, Harry's *Bostonians* had been reviled—after it took him twice as many installments to finish as he'd planned. His publisher, James Osgood, had gone bankrupt.

My *East Angels*, on the other hand, though never a favorite of my male critics, was poised to enjoy a great success in *Harper's*. Neither Howells nor Harry believed in the grief that sustained my heroine, Margaret. I had given her a cad of a husband, inspired by my brother Charley, with a dash of King's charisma. She lived with pain, as did I, though our heartaches were different. My health was not improving. The London crowds, the bleak winter, the cold, were weighing upon me. The completion of a project always left a hole in my heart, causing me to move. This time, I decided to move south.

February 25, 1886

Dear Alice:

It is with strong—mixed—emotion that I write to tell you of my plans to leave England for southern parts within the fortnight.

I say "mixed" because my heart sings at the prospect of Italian warmth and sun. The English damp has not been optimal for my health, nor have the English doctors succeeded in relieving my pain. Since the heat has always provided relief, and the talented Dr. Baldwin, of whom I've spoken to you, are in Florence, I will make my way there.

I also confess that my soul could do with a bit less of British society and its chasm between high and low. Perhaps we Americans are on to something after all . . .

But it does pain me to bid farewell to you and to Miss Loring. How enriched I have been by our ties together at Leamington. Female companionship is truer than any.

You know better than anyone how the body can interfere with the mind. Keep me in your thoughts and write to me often. How marvelous it would be to see you both in Italy at summer's end!

With affection,
Connie

I have this letter in my possession because it was returned to me with one line scratched upon it:

C—If my brother Harry follows you, I will stop eating.

A.

CHAPTER SEVEN

The Truth about Harry

"I found a house at Florence on the hill of Bellos-guardo." Because of Mrs. Browning's *Aurora Leigh*, many have imagined this dream, and figure they know it well enough.

But I did find a house all my own on the hill of Bellosguardo, and my happiness there surpassed anything I had read about in poetry or fiction. The contentment did not depend on the glorious views of the valley, the mountains that change from campanile-studded plummy Appenines to white Carrara, the winding Arno . . . nor was it only because of the cypress trees, the scent of olives, the golden hillside color so peculiar to Tuscany . . . nor did it rest in my enchanting rooms, each—including the writing room—with a view, the talent of my cook, the graciousness of my neighbors. No, in my house on the hill of Bellosguardo I found something I had sought my whole life—a complete harmony among work and beauty and other people. Through my earnings, my own hard work and success, I was able to create for myself the life I had always wanted. In my imagination I still hold tight to my Florentine time, despite everything that happened there.

After the damp dramas of England, my return to Florence was a sweet homecoming. The little American and English community, such as it was, welcomed me with open arms. Dr. Baldwin, comforting soul, was happy to have me nearer at hand, and gave me great assurances that my condition was at the least stabilizing. Most importantly, the art and the churches and the alleys and the crevices greeted me, saying, Signora Woolson, throw away that *Baedaker!* You don't need it any more. We are yours. And they were right—I had finally crossed the line from tourist to *cognoscenta.*

When I first arrived, I stayed in town at the Hôtel de l'Arno to get my bearings. But I yearned for a real house, near enough to the center but apart from society, ideally to be situated in one of the picturesque hill towns. Among the more interesting friends I had made through Harry were the Bootts—Francis Boott and his daughter Lizzie, who traveled in tow with Frank Duveneck, Lizzie's painting teacher, mentor, and for years (many of us assumed), lover. When I returned to Florence in 1886, Lizzie and Frank had married, old Mr. Boott having finally given the union his official blessing. They were not an unhappy trio, ensconced in two floors of the Villa Castellani in the town of Bellosguardo. In fact, it soon became apparent that the forty-year-old Lizzie was pregnant and more aglow than any twenty-five-year-old mother. These lovely friends, who understood exactly what I required in the way of comfort—and never questioned the wisdom of a woman living alone—set out to help me find a house in Bellosguardo. After all, they proclaimed, how could I not find inspiration in the town that had been home to Hawthorne when he wrote the *The Marble Faun*.

And so we found the Villa Brichieri, set in the most perfect of hills, with views that bettered even Mrs. Browning's. As the house was being readied for me, wouldn't you know that Harry descended upon Florence! Even my deaf ears could hear the Renaissance trumpets blaring as he made himself known to all of us. Even though he had just bought his own flat in London in DeVere Gardens, he found himself yearning for Italy. For three weeks in January he actually stayed at my not-yet-ready villa. He claimed he was watching it for me. I think he wanted to save the cost of his hotel.

Or as Lizzie said, her arms resting on her huge tummy, her feet up in front of the fire one night, "He keeps telling me he knows that you miss him too much and he owes you the solace of his company. Is he insane?"

"No, it's just the only way he has of saying that he needed a break from his sister Alice. Also that he missed the ease of being with his friends. Very social people are the loneliest of all, I think." I smiled at her. "You know, he says the same about you—that you miss him too much and he owes you the pleasure of his company, in your confinement."

This made her laugh so loud that Duveneck, her adoring Milwaukee-born artist husband, came running into the sitting room to be sure she hadn't gone into labor. "No," she assured him, "Connie here is just explaining to me the code of deciphering what Harry James means—she's very good at it. Seems the trick is to remember he usually means the opposite of what he says."

Dear Harry left us for Venice and the charms of his friend Mrs. Bronson. And just as Lizzie gave birth to a lovely little boy, I took possession of the Villa Brichieri, complete with Angelo the cook (and watchman) and a day servant.

Every morning I'd rise in the burnished chill of a Tuscan morning, gaze down into the valley, and say, "Connie, look at what you've done for yourself."

To walk with a steaming coffee at dawn, to stretch one's legs on a terrace overlooking the stony glory of Florence erupting around her curvaceous Arno, to be greeted by a desk on which a Renaissance lord wrote his wills and his love poems . . . that is heaven. I had companionship when I wanted it—in the evenings or on the village's visiting day. The response to *East Angels*, the Florida novel that King had urged me to write, was enthusiastic, so I even had the fleeting pleasure of critical validation. All I missed was a dog—a yearning that Angelo was more than happy to satisfy by lending his son's dog, Pax.

Into this heaven, Harry came.

The letters from Venice had become somewhat agitated—there were reasons, impossible to explain without compromising the most gracious of acquaintances, that he would prefer to leave the water city and return to Florence. But how could he remain in town when his beloved Lizzie and Fenimore were up in the hills? I took this to mean that some female had misinterpreted his attentions, though now I wonder if something else transpired ... and, that he wanted to stay in my villa. So, of course, I invited him to come—he could have an entire floor to himself.

If written correspondence can seem loud, his did. This was too great an imposition, he couldn't possibly, but if he were to stay, no one was to know, would he have an eastern view, what about the cook—would he also prepare meals for Harry? And remember, no one was to know. He did not, after all, want to compromise me in any way.

Ah, Harry, I was happy to give you all the privacy you needed.

So, my friend moved into the ground floor of my villa. Our days took on a very happy rhythm. We would both work in the mornings, in our separate rooms, and join each other for one of Angelo's delicious lunches. Most days I would walk, and Harry would nap. Some afternoons we went into town. There was the occasional dinner, but we usually confined ourselves to the Bootts or Mrs. Greenough or other Bellosguardo residents.

One glorious twilight I was walking up the hill to return to the villa. In my walk I'd gone further than usual and hadn't found my usual sidecut to the road. Through a gnarl of olive trees I made my way. I tucked up my outer skirts for old time's sake, just as I had when I was a girl. Though by then it was almost impossible for me to hear soft sounds like the rustling of leaves, I stood by a row of cypress trees and swayed with them, imagining that I could hear the whoosh of the soft fir branches moving as one.

I opened the rusty gate at the base of our garden. Up on the terrace where two figures, one sitting, one on the ground. Harry and some acolyte, I thought, and almost waved. But I decided to get closer first.

The sun was slanting low as I climbed closer. Harry was indeed sitting at the outdoor table, leaning back with his eyes closed, enjoying the warmth on his face.

But it was not an admirer of fiction sitting at Henry's feet. No, it was my cook's teenage son, Giorgio, who was on his knees before the master. And he seemed to be generating a different kind of heat in Harry's lap.

I sought the cover of a tree. Awash in the scent of lavender and thyme, I smiled. To know that Harry was human after all, that he allowed himself the expression of his own desires, filled me with a kind of awe.

And, of course, shock. Though of course I had heard of "aesthetes" and "inverts," I had never witnessed any such display of affection between two men, other than in my Parisian outings with King. Then the boys were painted like carnival performers. Suddenly I was a twelve-year-old girl again, peering around the side of the house with my brother Charley, to watch our dog mount the neighbor's retriever. I did not want to disturb Harry and yet I confess I was curious to see how matters would conclude. When I peered around my tree, Harry was cradling the lithe fellow in his arms and was kissing him. His large soft hand caressed Giorgio's brown cheek. The tenderness of the gesture swelled my heart.

I wanted to be happy for Harry. But now I possessed the dark thrill of a secret about this most private of persons.

I turned and made my way down the incline and found the outlet to the road. Though it was dusk, I was not afraid. The working men returning home from the farms and the quarries, and the leatherworkers, the children returning from school and play, the shop girls weary from their day of waiting on tourists in the center, must have been bemused at the sight of the middle-aged American woman, smiling.

That night, we were attending a dinner party at the Bootts. Harry arrived late in a velvet cloak, having first attended a reception in town. To watch Harry move in society was a wonder not of nature but of art, a dance worthy of the Royal Ballet. Now he was also lit bright from within. So many glasses of luscious local Chianti passed his lips that they were stained red. While I was asking Lizzie about baby Francis, he came from behind and put his arm around my waist.

"How well you look, Harry," observed Lizzie.

"Setting up house with *La Litteratrice* suits me," he said, too loudly. "Perhaps she shall cure me of my bachelor ways?"

I felt his breath on my neck. I found myself thinking that it was a good thing that Giorgio wasn't watching. "Harry thinks he can get away with saying anything in front of me because of my poor hearing," I laughed, extracting myself from his embrace. "He forgets that I still hear most anything. And that I am a devoted spinster, through and through."

Lizzie squeezed my hand. She whispered so that I had to lip read. "What if he really wants to marry you?"

Poor Lizzie didn't understand that was the last thing I wanted. To forever relegate my talents to second-class status, next to the master. And to give up my freedom so that he could pursue the young men he desired? Never.

Our days passed happily enough. He had begun to work on *The Aspern Papers*—with which he later punished me by creating the character of a lonely spinster, wooed for the papers of her aunt's literary lover. I was working on *Jupiter Lights*, returning to my Florida of freed slaves and misplaced souls.

One evening, we strolled out to the terrace. Though it was spring, a crisp autumnal chill had seized our hillside under the cover of evening. I held my wrap tightly around me. Harry had a brandy in his hand.

The moon was full, spilling her light over the houses in the valley, where lamps flickered in the windows.

"Firenze. We met here, did we not, Fenimore?"

"We did, Harry. You weren't so keen at first. But then you realized you had the ideal audience in me—a woman clever enough to understand you, but female enough not to fight back."

He laughed. "You wicked woman. Not fight back? Why, you are the most argumentative creature I've ever known. And you're far more than an audience.

You're my consigliere. And I hope I can be the same for you."

"*D'accordo*, Harry. I treasure you. Always."

"We do pretty well together, don't we?" he said, with a look that was almost coy. I had never seen such an expression on his face.

"We do," I answered. "You've fulfilled my dreams, Harry. You're the friend I always wanted—the artist with whom I can confide my dreams, my aspirations, my thoughts. So," I stopped.

"So?" he intoned slowly.

"So, know that you don't need to hide anything from me."

"What do you mean, Fenimore? I hide nothing from you. You have heard of my innermost demons."

"The boys, Harry. Giorgio. You don't need to sneak around. He can stay in your room. It doesn't bother me."

"I don't know what you're talking about." He swallowed what remained in the brandy snifter in one huge gulp.

"Harry, I saw you. I was coming up the hill."

He turned away from me and walked to the edge of the terrace. I followed him and reached for his elbow, but he shook it away.

"Harry, we are the best of friends," I pressed. "I trust you as my soulmate. I have nothing but affection and regard for you."

"You are inferring the most unsavory and disgraceful behavior to me. As if I were some sort of aesthete."

"That's not how I see it."

"It changes everything."

"It changes nothing." I positioned myself between him and the balustrade, so that he'd have to look at me. "Harry, it changes nothing. Just as I expect my private life to change nothing between us. 'It is possible to do everything both with caution and with confidence,' says our friend Epictetus."

"What exactly do you want from me? Am I supposed to be your consort now, your husband-to-be?"

He could not have slapped me and stung me more. "Are you mad?" I said quietly. "I have no interest in anything of the kind. We are friends."

"Whatever you are thinking, I cannot pay the price." His face had lost all its lovable softness and gone rigid, hard. "It is late. I shall retire now."

"Harry—"

"Without discretion, there is no freedom. Remember?" He made a small bow. "Though of course, I suppose you would rather one lived like your heroines, suffocated by longing and passion unrealized."

"Do you really know so little of me, Harry?"

"Good night, Fenimore. I shall continue to thank you for your most complete discretion."

The next morning, I was too agitated to write at my desk. Instead, I took a frantic, unjoyful walk among the olive trees, hoping to join Harry for coffee.

But when I returned to the villa, he was gone.

CHAPTER EIGHT

A Portrait of Miss Woolson

It turned out that, whatever his original intentions, Harry had already set in motion a most wicked gesture of thanks. After his disappearance that morning, I rifled through the papers on my desk, stopping at the February issue of *Harper's* that was proudly opened to the page with Harry's byline. I picked up the magazine, hungry for a reminder that my angry friend had shown affection and respect for me in such a public forum. But as I reread the essay that had prompted our sharing of a bottle of champagne just a month earlier, I saw it with new eyes—as if I were reading it translated into my native tongue for the first time.

It was an article of appreciation entitled "Miss Woolson," by the esteemed author of *The Portrait of a Lady*. And under the pretense of admiring my work, the master did nothing other than make it seem small, and local, and—worst of all—female.

As I read the catalog of my minor triumphs, I sank to the ground. For line by line, he had created a cunning portrait not of a body of work, but of the character of their creator. No one could leave that essay with any impression other than that Miss Woolson was herself a long-suffering, martyred spinster who had spent too much time in unsavory and exotic American locales. For what did he applaud?

My talent rendering local scenes, from the icy straits of Mackinac to the unsung, postwar South, with a "sympathy altogether feminine." My "impressions gathered in the course of lonely afternoon walks at the end of hot days," a personal habit known to Harry only through our most intimate conversations.

My Negroes, "philological studies" worthy of Uncle Remus. Not flesh and blood people—Harry couldn't imagine such a thing.

My predilection for cases of heroic sacrifice— "sometimes unsuspected, and always unappreciated." According to Harry, I was fond of people who've given up the memory of happiness, who "love and suffer in silence."

The master of the inner life commented on my apparent interest in the "inner life" of the "weak, the superfluous, the disappointed, the bereaved, the unmarried." Though he noted, like the rest of my sex, I like "marriages even better."

My (supposed) taste for little country churches and geneology and picturesque, as representing us as "we would like to be."

And worst of all—the man to whom I had bared my soul about the predicament of being female, about my desire to be mistress of my own fate and fortune—this very same confidant described me as someone fundamentally conservative—smugly asserting that I would never lend my voice to a "revolution that should place my sex in the thick of the struggle for power."

Only someone determined to ignore my stories of struggling female artists, like "Miss Grief"—the best of my work—would conclude that for Miss Woolson, the "life of a woman is essentially an affair of private relations." Harry omitted any reference to the very tales that he had told me time and again represented my greatest achievement—the tales of struggling female artists. Instead, I was an "excellent example of the way the door stands open between the personal life of American women and the immeasurable world of print."

Ah, Harry, I knew what you were trying to do. You wanted the world to think that you were bestowing a great favor upon me. But nothing could have hurt more than those words of faint praise. It was no accident that you published this essay in the same magazine that had provided such a welcome home for my own writing.

I don't know how long I'd been there, tangled in my dress on the polished floor, when Angelo found me crying.

"*Signora, non preoccuparla. Signor James ritornera.*"

I waved him away. As I grabbed the edge of the desk to lift myself off the ground, the irony was not lost on me. For the rest of my days, the servants would talk about how I'd wept when Mr. James left me. They would never realize that it was his nasty little article that broke my heart.

Thus began the summer of the silent dreams.

My dreams, then and now, are noisy, loud affairs. People speak clearly, birds sing, music flares. But when

Harry left Bellosguardo, my sleep went as silent as he did. The result was terrifying. I would rise in the morning, afraid that my hearing had finally left me altogether. For several weeks I shunned even the company of dear Lizzie Boott, who had the wisdom to let me be. Dr. Baldwin's visits and invitations were rebuffed. I'm afraid I sank into a despair, and allowed my dearest friends to worry.

Until one night Father returned.

We were together in a skiff in the swampy waterways outside St. Augustine—where, of course, we had never been together. Father sat facing me as I maneuvered the boat in and around the dense rooted waterway, steering with my oar, sliding in between the hanging branches and leaves. I was so very happy to see him. He was wearing a beautiful straw hat, just as he used to during our summers at Mackinac.

We came to a narrowing of the river. Suddenly the animals—the cicadas and the birds, the frogs and the rattlesnakes—let loose in a cacophony of sound. An alligator snapped his mouth from the shore. I stopped, my oar mid-stroke.

"Connie, I didn't raise you to be a quitter. You have to keep on going, girl."

"But Papa, there's a gator on the shore."

"So what? Michael row the boat ashore. Allelujah."

And as Father sang the spiritual that Old Billy sang at Mother's funeral, the gator started to laugh.

I woke up knowing what I had to do. The battle of the stories was on.

Finally, I knew how to end my old story, "In the Chateau of Corinne"—the one that I had held back from *Harper's* all those years ago. Now, more than ever, it was clear to me that the husband needed to silence his poet-writing bride in order to control her.

I owe that much to Harry. For who else's voice did I hear when I invented my male character's rebuke of his wife's poetry, "A woman should not dare in that way. Thinking to soar, she invariably descends . . . A man feels like going to her, poor mistaken sibyl that she is, closing her lips with gentle hand, and leading her away to some far spot about the quiet fields, where she can learn her error, and begin her life anew"?

The truth is that I never held any illusions about my talent compared to Harry's. I was Salieri to his Mozart. But genius or not, my sanity depended on working. Without my routine—sorting through notes, thinking, beginning; the joy of ink on paper, blotting, scratching—the rest of my days were empty. Those

few hours of work gave shape to my day, freeing me
to walk, and eat, and drink . . . and even to savor the
rare company of others.

Papa was right. I couldn't be a quitter.

Angelo was overjoyed to see the return of my
appetite, complete with demands for *papardelle ai
funghi, coniglio allo cacciatore*, and other hearty dishes.
Dr. Baldwin, always alert to any connection between
my moods and the trouble in my ears, was happy to
see my spirits return. He had warned me on several
occasions that he feared my need to write bordered
on obsessive, since I could not tolerate interrup-
tions in my routine. Even the most natural changes
or diversions led to dire bouts of melancholia. Dr.
Baldwin was reading several French articles about
compulsion that he offered to share with me. Instead,
I turned again to *Jupiter Lights*, working with fresh
confidence.

As fall's breezes began to bring new strength,
I received a package forwarded care of my German
agents. I opened a box to find an inscribed copy of
Harry's *The Aspern Papers*. The note pinned to the
first page only noted, "With thanks for the creative
sojourn provided in Bellosguardo, HJ." I sat on the
terrace overlooking the Arno with a tray of Angelo's

biscotti and read without stop. How Harry loved his tales of literary reputation—this time in the shape of a fictional biographer who seeks the papers of his favorite poet, and is offered a Faustian bargain—marry the wretched, middle-aged niece of the poet's former lover, who has been hiding the treasure trove of letters, and the papers will be his. I knew all too well that many would see none other than Miss Woolson in the desperately housebound Miss Tina. I laughed out loud and scribbled a note to Harry, "Dear master, only a confirmed bachelor would cling to the notion that every unmarried woman is desperate to wed. After all, your lodger is hardly such a catch!" I had agreed to break the ice, and our correspondence resumed, though on somewhat tender footing.

When Katherine Loring left for winter in the States, leaving Alice to his care, he moaned that he could not be the sole angel of mercy. I ignored his hints that I visit England, though I wrote to Alice and invited her to visit Bellosguardo. I promised the perfumed air and the hills and the light would do her a world of good. I knew of course that her brother would never trouble to bring her there.

Her response would have made me laugh if it didn't reveal such deep unhappiness:

Dear Connie:

You're not the first woman to try to please my brother Harry by extending invitations to me. It's obvious that I can't trot around the continent like certain she-novelists. Furthermore, Harry would never allow it.

So, stop trying to seduce him.

Life without Katherine is unbearable. I hope I live until her return.

Won't you come back to England? Without Katherine here to read your stories to me, je suis desole.

Your devoted friend, Alice

Was I dismayed by what I learned about Harry? Did I want him for my own?

No. That is what people see. That is what they will say when I am gone. But any woman could tell you that Harry never once lit a spark of romance with a woman. Oh, I encouraged him to pursue women, as did his other friends. It was a conceit that his dignity demanded.

Of course, I had plenty of secrets of my own. But Harry never saw them for what they were. The sad truth is that after Bellosguardo, I would never be completely certain whether it was my company he craved, or my discretion.

CHAPTER NINE

Our Tragic Muses

*I*s a friend the person who knows your darkest secrets, or the one from whom you feel obliged to hide the worst? Once you care about someone's good opinion, are you ever free to reveal the truth? As you learn what is too much for a particular person to bear—Mary can't manage illness, sad Sue is helpless at affairs of the heart, barren Rachel can't abide talk of other people's children—don't you choose what to reveal and what to conceal?

Do you ever trust someone once he knows the worst?

The summer I was twelve years old I learned all too well the power of secrets. My brother Charley had taken to wandering in and out of the grandest summer houses on Mackinac Island in the late afternoon, when most people were out boating or walking or, most likely, napping in the cool shade of curtained upstairs bedrooms. His petty thievery was usually limited to food, though as the season wore on he was emboldened to take a shovel here, a hoe there, a bucket there. One morning Charley led me to the cave where he was accumulating his wares. I was astonished to see the variety he had assembled. "Whatever will you do with it all?" I asked, in shock. He just shrugged and made me promise never to tell.

I kept our secret until the end of August, when word came out that the Gossers had fired their Indian caretaker Philippe, blaming him for stealing a bridle. Philippe had always been kind to us children, giving us apples and handfuls of cherries.

"You must tell, Charley," I implored. He refused.

In despair, I went to my father, who listened calmly and thanked me for my honesty. For days after, you could spy Charley knocking on the doors of the people he had robbed, hammer or hoe or a cake from our kitchen in hand. His humiliation was so severe that he became incapable of looking anyone in the eye. When I heard him talking to himself in the tree behind our house, I shook with fear. Had I done the right thing?

I never told Charley I was the one who had revealed his secret. But I did try to buy his trust by offering him a secret in return. I told him that I kept a private diary, in which I chronicled ugly truths about our family and friends. I showed him the leatherbound book and its hiding place under a rock near my favorite cove. But, of course, once I had shown it to him, I never kept it there again.

The strength I had been finding in work and routine evaporated in the winter of 1888. In March I received word that my beloved friend Lizzie Boott had died of pneumonia while visiting Paris with her husband and baby boy. The extinguishing of that light darkened my days on the hill of Bellosguardo. Weeping, I watched the heartbroken father and husband pack up their belongings to leave Italy forever. My circle on the hill was shrinking.

Harry's letters, which had regained some of their taunting familiarity, began to arrive with alarming frequency. The veneer of confidence had evaporated with the shock of losing Lizzie and the failure of both *The*

Bostonians and *Princess Casamassima*. At last he released himself from the chains of propriety and reserve. If only he and I could see each other, it would restore his spirits. If only he could leave London and meet me in Europe. If only it would not be scandalous to travel together, as two unattached and desirable adults.

I read on, and thought: if only you did not fear what I know about you.

Suffocating in the heat of that sorrowful Italian summer, my American soul began to yearn for the balm of a place both prosperous and protestant. I concocted a scheme to go to Switzerland—but not alone. To equal the score between us, I offered Harry a secret we could share. I wrote to him with the "news" that I was planning an illicit rendezvous with a certain male acquaintance, and would welcome his presence as a shield against gossip. Could he look ahead to a time when he would be free for a mutual holiday? Could we meet in Geneva, and tell no one?

Harry, dear Harry, took the bait like a wall-eyed trout biting one of old man Pierre's special lines back home. Within weeks we had booked hotels on either side of Lake Geneva. My trunk and I arrived at the end of September. I stood on the terrace of my modest hotel, smiling at the spectacular blue, the sculpted white mountains. Of course the only man I was planning to see in Geneva was Harry. What I didn't know was that we would end up staying for two months.

You might say that this elaborate ruse was the end of my true friendship with Harry. But I think of it more as a beginning. Though I had given him my false secret to protect, I kept many other vital truths from him, ranging from the real men who figured in my intimate life (including King) to the agony of my health. Ultimately, I denied Harry the chance to prove himself as a true support to me in times of need. Instead, I gave myself what I wanted: the freedom to be with him. I was selfish. I gave him up, in order to have him, even if it was on the terms that kept him comfortable. I allowed him to think that I needed him, which freed him to need me.

Within days of our arrival we developed our Swiss routine, as punctual as the bourgeois citizens, as tidy as their streets. I would rise at dawn and work until noon, followed by a simple lunch and a brisk, healthful walk—or, most heavenly, a row on the lake. In late afternoon I would take a paddle steamer to whichever spot we had appointed the day before—most usually, the Jardin Anglais on the Rive Gauche. We would

meander through the Old Town, perhaps stopping at
a café, often talking of our shared sorrows. Lizzie's
loss. We usually dined together before I returned to
my hotel, and Harry set off for his rooms at Hotel de
l'Ecu. A peculiar choice of venue, since he had apparently spent a miserable year there in his youth when
his father sent him to the mathematical institute while
William studied at the university.

One late October day he was sitting in an armchair in the dark of his hotel lobby. He frowned at
the letter he had just read, folded it, and placed it in
his vest pocket.

"Alice is agitated," he said as we walked into the
blinding blue of the afternoon.

"Does she know where you are?"

"Why no—I was after all asked to protect the
privacy of a friend, whose honor and virtue I hold
dear."

"Since she and I do have a companionable friendship, Harry, I think it would be fine to mention that
I am here."

He put a thick finger to his lips as if to silence
me, and smiled.

"You have never asked me, Harry, with whom I
spend my afternoons and the occasional evening."

"As long as it is not that abominable Clarence King—who I happen to know is in Mexico, spending more of John Hay's money searching for precious metals—it is none of my affair. I rather enjoy the idea of your *liaisons dangereuses*. Let me fancy that it is a Swiss aristocrat who leaves you so happy, not a factory magnate from Cleveland."

I laughed.

He never mentioned what had happened in Bellosguardo—what I had seen or the explosion that had torn through our friendship like the dynamite in King's mines when I confronted him that terrible evening. I didn't want to risk capsizing that little boat of Jamesian tranquillity that I had labored so hard to construct. Therefore, I contrived to get to his innermost thoughts via his favorite subject: his work.

"*The Aspern Papers* is very clever, Harry. Last evening I was rereading the copy you gave me. I like to think of you working on it in Italy when we were together."

We were by now in the Place du Bourg-de-Four, whose fancy shop windows had become a regular destination in our daily excursions.

"It was inspired by that story Eugene Lee-Hamilton told me, about Claire Clairmont and that supposed cache of Shelley letters she was guarding so violently. A mad old woman. But it is a subject that haunts me. The invasion of an artist's privacy, that is."

"You mean the work should live on its own terms, without eliciting any curiosity in the writer's personality?" I pointed to a table at one of our regular café stops.

He shook his head, no. We reversed our course and strolled back in the direction of the water. I breathed the perfume of pastry and warm cheese and regretted his restlessness. French and German pattered around us.

"Of course."

"That's not very modern and romantic of you, Harry. And I dare say you don't really practice what you preach. After all—why mention my daily walks in your essay 'Miss Woolson' if they have no relation to my work?"

It was a shot I could not resist drawing with my bow. Private relations, affairs of the heart, he could have. But not my work.

"But that's the ineffable dilemma of it, don't you see, Connie? It is impossible to put aside what one knows—once it's there."

We walked in silence, the street sloping down to the water. The lamps were being lit. Ahead the luminous twilight blue of the lake glowed between the buildings. Then one of the infernal stabs of pain shot through the left side of my head. For a second I lost my balance and had to lean against the corner of a bank.

"Are you engaged this evening, *mia litteratrice?*" he asked.

"Not until much later," I lied, still trying to steady myself. As we continued, I felt as if I were at sea, crossing the Atlantic again.

"Perhaps, then, we shall dine at my hotel. But first, let's rest at that café in the Jardin that you liked so much the other day."

I nodded. Though I could not feel my legs beneath the weight of my skirts, I allowed him to usher me to a table overlooking the water. Lights blinked across the lake.

"Remarkable how popular that blasted fountain is," he said, frowning at the Jeu d'Eau that shot up like a whale's spray from the harbor. "I much preferred the view without it."

"I like its straightforwardness," I said. "It seems right for the Swiss."

"Perhaps, perhaps . . . and how my Midwestern Connie likes her straightforwardness. That is why few things matter as much as communication between us, Fenimore," he said, as the waiter poured my tea. "Our society provides something precious, worth protecting at all cost. And yet . . ."

Perhaps the dizziness was due to hunger, I thought, gripping tight to the curved arm of my chair as another wave swept through me.

"Yet what, Harry?" I managed to say.

"One is haunted by the fear that in the wrong hands, the most intimate communication might be misconstrued."

"Whose hands are the wrong hands?" I took his brandy glass and sipped it to quell my queasiness. He didn't take any notice.

"After we are gone."

"Oh, Harry, really! How morbid! You must conquer this fear of death. When we are gone, let the world have its fun. No one will care about me—but you, you will be studied. Perhaps someone, some crafty scholar, will imagine that we were lovers?"

His face drained white, like the spray of the Jeu.

"You needn't look so horrified, Harry. It's not the worst fate that could befall you." I took another gulp of his brandy, which having the desired effect.

"Of course not—in fact, it's brilliant. Do you think we should?"

"Should what?"

"Wed, Fenimore. If we were to wed, we would protect each other in the eyes of history, but allow each other, umm, a unique privacy during our lives. Just as we're doing here in Geneva."

I didn't realize how tightly the net of worry held his features in place until I saw the grip loosen at that moment. He looked so hopeful, so free.

But I knew it was a disastrous idea. My chest closed at the very thought. A month's holiday was one thing. A life built around a lie—another.

"Harry," I said, placing my hand on his. "That is not a good idea, for either of us. Or for our work."

The net retightened.

"Harry, you can never control what others think. You should know that by now."

"Then you must promise me—"

"What?"

"I want you to promise me that you will burn my letters," he said.

I thought of my precious boxes, that moved with me from country to country, lease to lease, packed tight with my correspondence, not only with Harry but

with other great men of my day. A different colored
ribbon held the letters of each man: blue for Harry, red
for John Hay, pink for King, green for Dr. Baldwin. It
may not sound very modern, but this tangible proof
of their interest in my friendship, my thoughts, made
me feel alive.

"But I treasure your letters, Harry. I return to my
favorites when I am low. You know how vital they are
to me, to my health."

"Of course you may continue to keep them now,
my friend. But before you leave this earth, I would like
you to destroy them."

"What makes you so certain that any of us knows
the precise moment we will leave this earth, Harry?"
Though I am beginning to think that I will know mine,
I thought, and it will be far sooner than yours.

"Then simply provide for the same in your estate." He leaned forward. "Will you promise? It will
be our secret."

I had no intention of obliging him, of course. But
I feared that if I refused, I would no longer savor his
freest expressions of doubt and concern and affection,
his deepest thoughts about his art and his work.

And so, not for the first time that Swiss autumn,
I lied.

CHAPTER TEN

Confessions

$\mathscr{I}$ did have another secret, a shameful one. I tried to experience my pain, to know it and even to make it my friend. Over and again I read my Epictetus for guidance, seeking the strength to command my body with my reason. But I was weak. And the pain grew fiercer.

In Geneva, the loss of balance frightened me. But I did not want to confide in Harry. I knew how he recoiled from the unseemly betrayals of the body. Time and again I had witnessed his aversion to the illnesses of others—his sister Alice once said that the only physical malady that could ever capture Henry's true sympathy was the one that began with lunch and ended in his own digestive tract. So, I sought assistance from a doctor who had been recommended by the hotel concierge.

"Why should Madame suffer?" smiled Dr. Schneider, his pink cheeks almost as shiny as his pomaded hair. He handed me my first glass-stoppered bottle. "She is entering a time of life when many women struggle with a disordered mind." He waved away my explanation that I had suffered this pain, now worsening, for twenty years.

In the privacy of my room, I dropped just a hint of the brownish red liquid into a glass of water. It stank of bitter licorice. I gulped it down like lemonade on a hot Mackinac summer's day, and waited for it to help me. At first, I felt nothing. Then, a cramping queasiness in my stomach. And then, as the room began to glow, I surrendered to its spell.

No, I am not the first or the last to wrestle with this devil. But, I am ashamed to say, I approached the taking of laudanum with the same plodding determination I had previously devoted to my health. I am nothing if not a creature of routine—and so now I created a new, secret routine. As a result, the laudanum almost took me. Not just my body—my strong, athletic body—but my soul.

Solitude invites discipline—and just as easily, dissolution. Just as no one is there to witness the widower taking his gin at three in the afternoon rather than at the sociable hour, or to stop the lonely traveler from eating dinner at five instead of seven, no one was present in my bedroom to stop my hand when I reached for the bottle. At first it was just a foot on the pedal of the piano, dampening and muffling my thoughts. And then the erratic pain, the fear and the worry, would dance like musical notes, complete with chords and arpeggios, and build into a crescendo of release. The fist of pain in my head relaxed, the fingers stretched one by one, and the warmth rushed through me. As I strengthened the dose, I was given spots of clarity, insight. Worlds became clear. Or so I thought. Though I never once drank the vile liquid before seeing Henry James, I began to try it before venturing out into the world on my own.

My last day in Geneva I was alone. Harry had departed. I sat by the lake on one of the beautiful benches, twirling my parasol.

"In a minute, mama," called a young girl, absorbed in the book on her lap. A ribboned auburn plait hung down the back of a simple modern blue dress. She was that precarious age, suspended between girlishness and womanhood, that might last two days or two years. Just as she slammed the book shut, a Westmoreland terrier jumped into her lap. The girl squeezed the little white dog so hard she might have choked it. The expression of love on her face was pure. A man, perhaps her father, gently removed the dog to the ground.

The girl was me. My younger self, stripped of the years of worldly experience that had taught me to twist emotions into secrets and honest gestures into lies.

"Let her be!" I screamed. Stern European faces turned toward me. "She has so little time to love her dog," I shouted. Sobs shook my body.

"Does Madame need help? Perhaps she is not well?" asked the man who had taken the dog from the girl's lap. He stepped toward me.

I sliced my parasol through the air like a boy wielding a toy sword. Then I threw it on the ground, turned, and staggered away from him. In a dreamlike state I found my way back to the hotel. I don't remember the attendant helping me to pack, but I think I left for Florence the next day, or the day after.

I did fill several Swiss prescriptions before I left to return to Italy. Ultimately, the only thing one can do with laudanum is run out.

The knife in my head was not the only pain that the opiate helped to dull in that sad spring of 1889. Bellosguardo was now like an affable but unfaithful lover—the flush of blind infatuation was over, and the joys were all behind us. Now it was the place where Lizzie had died, the place where things had changed between Harry and me. My work on *Jupiter Lights* stalled. Never before had I been unable to write. Afraid to feel, laudanum became my only helpmate, if an untrustworthy one. For every afternoon that I spent lying on the chaise on the terrace, nodding at the view of Campanile and the cathedral, there would be at least one moment that tore my heart apart. An olive tree would sway like one of the dancers I'd seen in Paris with King. An apple sitting on a platter looked like Harry. A bird would rest on the rail and speak to me in my father's voice.

"I have failed you, Father," I moaned, rocking in my chair at noon one sunny day. "I have become weak." Angelo stood patiently, waiting for me to rise

and enter the house. I shuffled after him. A tureen of
simple vegetable soup steamed from the table where
Henry and I used to enjoy our lunches after long
creative mornings at our desk.

"What do you think you're doing?" I shouted.

"Trying to make Signora well again," he bowed.

I pushed my plate and cutlery to the floor. He
looked as if he would cry.

"I am so sorry, Angelo," I whispered. I retired to
my bedroom. The unfinished pages of *Jupiter Lights* sat
on my desk, a dry pen resting on top of them. I fell
on the bed, fully clothed.

When I awoke, a man was standing at the foot of
my bed. The only man in my life, other than King, who
was genuinely interested in truth, as far as I understood
it: Dr. Baldwin. He gave an embarrassed little bow and
extended a hand to help me stand.

"My dear Constance," he said, after I had splashed
my face with water in the basin. "You do not seem
well."

"I'm fine." I found the chair at my desk and sat
down, so that I could rest my head in my hand.

"When was the last time you took one of your
walks?" he asked. I had no answer. "Have you been
working every morning?" Again I was silent.

"I hesitate to ask another question, because of course you are free to seek another physician's care— a second opinion, as they say." He coughed. "But I worry—"

"Worry? About what?"

"I am afraid that you are using laudanum. I see the influence of morphine in your demeanor, your eyes, your behavior. Why, look here." He placed a sheaf of papers before me. The pages bled with thick, clotted ink.

"Constance, you wrote me five letters within the space of three days, all concerning the same subject: the failure of Henry James's most recent book, and the urgency of my visiting you, even though I had told you I would be in Siena until yesterday evening."

It seemed a month passed before I could look at him.

"The pain," I whispered.

"This vile narcotic does not cure the pain, it obscures it. How can we judge if there is any improvement?"

"But if I cannot sleep, I cannot work."

"You have not worked since you've returned from Switzerland." I realized in that moment what a friend I had in Angelo, my simple caretaker. "Did something happen there?"

"No," I murmured, "the pain just became too great for me. I was too dizzy to walk."

"There are new developments, marvels. I have read about something they call artificial eardrums. We will try them all. But you must free yourself from the grip of this narcotic. It brings on a despondency that is worse than the wilderness of pain. You can make your way through that wilderness. You are a pioneer, remember?"

I nodded. I rose and opened my armoire. From the back of a drawer I removed five small brown bottles and gave them to Dr. Baldwin.

"Constance, I promise you this: if it ever comes to pass that there is no hope—that there is no medical relief—I will help you. I will provide the prescriptions you need. But not now."

"Thank you for taking the trouble to address me with such honesty, my friend," I said. "It is not easy. But promise me you'll speak of this to no one."

He knew that I meant Harry. He nodded.

"I have two reasons to free myself from this chain," I said. "I need to finish *Jupiter Lights*. And I hope to travel to the East with my sister and niece, who arrive in three months' time."

"You may have a third reason," he smiled. "I believe that another good friend of yours will be here within the year."

He handed me several envelopes, the top with King's name and return P.O. box. My hand trembled. I fought the hollow hunger for the drug that shot through me.

"With your permission, I will stay here for several days," he said. "The withdrawal from the drug may make you ill, though I trust you are not so far along in your dependence on it."

I nodded my assent.

"And let's see what Angelo is preparing for supper, shall we?"

The stack of letters I had been ignoring included correspondence from Alice James, John Hay, Henry, my sister Clara—in short, all my very favorite people. But I confess that the one that I clung to during those next harrowing weeks was from that undaunted seeker of fortune, Clarence King.

My darling Cons:

How's my favorite writer? Giving the blokes a run for their money, I hope?

These blasted Mexican mines are like an overdue pregnant woman who can't go into labor. I know they hold more silver than anything I've yet tapped in Utah or California . . . but getting them to give it up is a beastly challenge. We need a different kind of processing machinery—details of which I won't bore you with, but suffice it to say it's more cash up front now, though more cash out down the road.

I know money isn't the kind of subject one discusses with a lady, but you're no regular lady—which I mean as the highest compliment. Life's kicked me in the ___ more than it's kicked most, but I carry on. What other choice do we have, after all . . . In the end there's just no logic to who succeeds and who fails, who finds happiness and who suffers. Look at our friend John Hay, enjoying in quiet masochistic misery the fortune of his unsympathetic wife. (I know she's the sister of your nephew's wife, but we talked about this in Paris so I write with a free hand here.) Or that cold fish Henry Adams, locked in a room writing those tedious books. Honestly, if I'd been married to him I'd have killed myself too, just like Clover did . . . Perhaps it's time he and your pal Henry James take a tour of the Orient together (!). If that's not clear, I'll explain when I see you next, my woman of the world.

Speaking of which—American financiers being the most short-sighted bunch of fools, I'm going to have to head across the Atlantic in search of capital when this Mexican tour is *done. I expect to be there next year—and whatever else is going on in your life, you minx, I hope we shall have some time together. Having traveled around the world and known its various pleasures, I feel compelled—not just by loneliness but by affection—to remind you how unique you are among your sex and race. I've never enjoyed so much private laughter with a white woman. And that's not the whiskey talking, dear Cons.*

Now finish another novel with all those wonderful characters so I can boast about you some more.

With deepest regard—and warmth,

King

It takes a lot to make one smile in the agonizing grip of withdrawal from laudanum. But every time I read King's letter, and thought of how Harry would react to the notion that I wasn't half bad, for a white woman, I laughed out loud.

CHAPTER ELEVEN

In the Shadow of the Pyramids

*S*ometimes the simple ministrations of an uncomprehending niece are the sweetest gift of all.

I looked at Clare, who was speaking quietly with the shipping agent. She had a detailed list of the Boott and Duveneck possessions that the grieving father and husband had left behind with me for safekeeping. Now I too was leaving Bellosguardo, and it was time to send them on. Frank, kind soul, wanted me to keep Mrs. Browning's chair, in honor of Lizzie. With all her Midwestern pragmatism Clare was determined that the Italian agent understand that it was this particular chair—the one with the special ribboned tag—that would join the possessions on the other list—the one that noted which of my possessions would be going into storage while she and I traveled to Greece and Egypt.

"Dear Clare, I think he understands. *Ha capito, signor?*"

The gentleman bowed and took the opportunity to scurry up to the kitchen, where Angelo would reward his patience with a morning cordial.

"I know, Aunt Connie, but honestly—a chair that belonged to Mrs. Browning, left to you by your friend. It's just too much. Sometimes I don't know how you can sit still in this fantastic place—views from every window, so much to see in town. I did one of Miss Horner's walks in Florence the other day and my mind was reeling."

"It's beautiful, I agree. But once you'd lived here a bit, like I have, you'd find it's the quieter beauties of day-to-day life that really make my heart sing." I took her hand and walked her out to the terrace.

"Even this house predates Columbus discovering America. Imagine!" She continued, "And then, centuries later, Ruskin's friend Miss Alexander lived here—the one he wrote about so much. Hawthorne lived down the road. To top it all off—Henry James used this same writing desk when he was living here, with you!"

My heart gave a little twist. "Well, don't forget that Angelo will be here to oversee the final move."

"Ah, Angelo. Can't we bring him back to New York? His cooking is better than Delmonico's and you pay him less a month than we'd have to pay a second-rate cook by the week at home."

"I don't think Angelo would find life in Manhattan as simpatico as life here, Clare. Besides, what he has really provided for me these past years has no price."

"Yes, Mama told me he took care of you when you were ill. How lucky you were to find a manservant who is so trustworthy. Mama says she'd be terrified to be alone in a house with fever and no one but a cook. She'd expect all her jewelry to be gone before the fever broke."

I didn't mention the long nights when it was Dr. Baldwin who bathed my brow and soothed my screams. But the truth was I'd trust Angelo with more than my few pieces of jewelry—and I had.

"Well, then, it's just as well that your mother is in town today, visiting the Smiths of Cleveland at their hotel, isn't it? I'd hate to think of her trying to eat while Angelo makes his way through her hatboxes."

Lovely Clare laughed so heartily, she warmed my soul.

ELIZABETH MAGUIRE

"So let's see what delights this paragon of the
kitchen has prepared for our lunch today, shall we?" I
said. She followed me into the dining room. A beautiful broth, in which floated a handful of homemade
tortellini and a few shreds of spinach, awaited us.

"Angelo! This will give me the strength to put
the finishing touches on *Jupiter Lights*. Perhaps I will
be done today. The family and I will be ready to
depart."

Angelo brushed a tear from his eye, mumbled
something about checking the roast veal, and left the
room.

Clara and Clare did not relish the prospect of
taking the fast train down the Adriatic coast—dubbed
the Indian Mail—as much as I did. We agreed that
they would make the southbound journey via Rome
with friends, and I would meet them in Brindisi.
There we would embark on the steamer that would
take us east for our journey to Greece and Egypt. Even
in my first-class compartment, the rustic pleasures of
the Indian Mail delighted me. Had I forgotten the
dangerous thrill of travel, the way it distracts one from
other heartaches? Arriving at Brindisi at midnight,
my fate depended on five local oarsmen who had to

row me out to the Austrian-Lloyd steamer that sat in the stream awaiting passengers. As the wind whipped our small boat, and the rowers shouted to each other in a dialect I could not understand, I was filled with a sense of calm. I was on water, again. And perhaps I could put the agonies of my final Florentine battles behind me.

The next morning I awoke in my red velvet cupboard of a cabin, and went in search of my niece and sister on the deck. We had passed the snowy caps of Albania and were entering a part of the sea that seemed to shimmer with light. Never had I experienced anything so completely, purely blue as the Ionian Sea.

"It is beautiful, is it not?" I said, embracing Clare.

"It is so bright, Aunt Connie," she squinted. "I don't know how to see it. It seems as if Mother doesn't quite like it." She nodded at Clara, sitting wrapped in a blanket on a deck chair. I gave my sister a kiss on the cheek. She smiled but waved me away to leave her in her seasickness.

I returned to the rail by my niece's side. "There is Corfu," I pointed to the island that rose before us, white hills and buildings, Greek and European, all a gorgeous jumble. "Our first stop. Do you remember our first water journey together, Clare, ten years ago? When we crossed the Atlantic together with your mother?"

"I do. It was terrifying to me—I was so young."

"Ten years is a long time. I was already middle-aged, but it seems like a lifetime ago. I was a girl myself in many ways."

"We didn't realize that you were running away for good, Aunt Connie. That you so wanted to get away from us all."

Her face puckered. I squeezed her hand.

"Not running away, my dear. Just seeking out the freedom to write, to make friendships based on affinity rather than on family. I had nursed my mother for many years, remember. That's the lot of the single daughter, no matter what her aspirations, literary or otherwise."

"Mother worries about you. She says you are subject to melancholia, just like your father. And that you should trust your family more, because no one will love you like we do." She lowered her face, afraid that she had told too much.

The steamer blew its horn. As we approached the harbor, we could make out the legion of small boats that waited to take passengers ashore, like a fleet of hansom cabs on water.

"I love my family, Clare. That's why you and your mother are here with me. And someday, I will return to America, and buy a house in Florida, so that I can sit like a fat old cat in the warmth of the sun, and all your children can come to visit and play in the waves of the sea." Still, I thought, I will never return to the tedious obligations of Cleveland or even New York.

"Until then, you needn't fear what you hear about melancholia—many of my generation are so afflicted, it is true," I went on, "the men as well as the women. I don't know if it was the war, or the anxieties of our age . . . our parents had no time to wallow. But we, we wrestle with demons. I am one of the lucky ones. My work always provides a way out."

"I won't get in the way of your work this trip, Aunt Connie. I promise."

"No chance of that, my dear, as the fees *Harper's* will pay me for my travel sketches will buy us many a handsome dinner!" I smiled. "Now, let's make sure our trunks are loaded onto a reliable-looking raft, shall we?"

From Corfu we made our way to Athens, and then to Cairo. Everything was so new, so wild, even to a seasoned traveler like myself. Clare and I developed that precious intimacy that draws together cabin mates or stagecoach riders as they sojourn in a strange land. Though I could negotiate the drivers and the tips and the concierges like a veteran, I was as new to Egyptian bazaars and camels and ruins as she was. I concentrated on my "Impressions" for *Harper's*, and earned a pretty penny in the process.

I suffered very few of the attacks that had plagued my trip to Geneva. Whether it was due to the therapeutic effect of the heat or just the mercurial nature of my disease, I shall never know. But freed from dizziness and the more acute attacks of pain, I found I had even more of my old energy than I'd reclaimed in Bellosguardo. Clare was happy to find her aunt a bit more sociable at dinner tables than she had expected. The evening of the Coptic Easter Monday, we actually joined an American party in our hotel and stood around a piano singing "Rally Round the Flag, Boys" and "The Star Spangled Banner." A very odd evening for me—a taste of Mackinac summer, in the shadow of the pyramids.

In Cairo, we were befriended by Brugsch Bey, the man who discovered the Pharoahs, and Professor Pierce of Harvard became my daily companion during the last weeks of my stay there. What a fascinating and sympathetic man. Like me, Professor Pierce had given

rein to his great passion—in his case, his newfound
Orientalism—in his middle years. He and I found com-
mon ground in the need for girls and boys to receive
equal educations . . . so that women and men can be
equal companions in life. Such conversations bored
Clare, despite my efforts to include her. She shopped
the bazaars with her mother, while Professor Pierce
and I rode donkeys together through the sites.

Of course, I had never been in a world that kept
women more separate than the land of the Arabs.

Looking back, I like this snippet from my Egyptian diary, and so I include it here, as it captures well
my mood:

I am like Flaubert—I love Egypt in all its color and cry.
But I think I would not like it so well if I were born here, and
forced to wear a heavy black veil, or to service fat Frenchmen
from a harem ripe with the stink of loveless love. Harry would
not care for the reek of camel and spice; or so he would protest
. . . but perhaps he could be free, here? I have caught the sweet
scent of the pipe from inner rooms denied to me. I long to try
it, but I dare not, given my promise to Dr. B.

And I did not, on that trip. But I confess that I
thought about it, as I lay in bed, listening to the soft

snores of my sister and her daughter in the adjoining room, trying to breathe away the flutter inside my head. The heat, the oiled massages of the attendants, the distraction of the sun and the white plaster and the tile and the turquoise sky, all provided a respite. Not the last of my life, but the last that would extend so long, and so comfortably.

Florida, I thought, might do just the same. And so the idea of an ultimate Florida retreat began to take root in my heart in a swampy, mangrove sort of way.

CHAPTER TWELVE

The Ambassador

"We Jameses do not like secrets, do we Katherine?" said Alice, pushing her torso to a sitting position amidst the many cushions of her chair in the parlor of their apartment at Leamington Spa. I always suspected there was far more strength in those little arms than anyone imagined.

"You do not, dear Alice, but that doesn't mean that the rest of the world has agreed to forgo the pleasure," answered Katherine. "More tea, Constance?"

I nodded and held out my cup to her.

"Why are you back in England? Are you chasing Harry?" challenged Alice.

This was one fantasy I wanted to put to rest. "Alice, you know as well as I do that your brother is not interested in a romantic attachment with me or anyone else."

"Constance, you know as well as I do that my brother needs the illusion that he is the object of women's romantic interest. As far as I can tell, his dignity depends on it. It allows him to live the life he wants to live."

"Well said, Alice. We all create the person we want to be, don't we?" said Katherine.

"Do you understand me, Constance?" pressed Alice.

"Yes, completely."

"So, then why are you here? Are you going to break my brother's heart?"

James Family, I wanted to shout, the world does not revolve around you.

"It's not within my power to break his heart, dear Alice, but even if it were, nothing could be further from what I want to do. He is my dear friend."

"Are you ill? Are those earaches flaring up again? Because if you are here to secure Dr. Baldwin's attention, you should abandon the thought. Even though Sir Clark attends to me, I also require Dr. Baldwin's time when he is in England. You see, I am about to begin dying, and it is a show that has one leading lady only. I will not share the stage this time. I've been in the chorus my whole life. Not now."

The truth was, I had returned to England partly on the advice of Dr. Baldwin. He was convinced that I would receive the best medical attention there . . . and that it would be healthy for me to work amidst a language and a culture more familiar than the Italian. I was also there to steal precious time with my old friend Clarence King. However, an assignation with King would never win the approval of Miss James—or Miss Loring.

"Alice, I would never take Dr. Baldwin away from you in your time of need. But pray do not threaten to die. We love you too much."

"Do you know that my father, ridiculously, gave me permission to kill myself when I was thirty years old? The fool debated the issue on abstract moral grounds, looking at the ceiling as if there were a sage speaking to him from the plaster work, while I lay writhing in my bed." She shook her head fiercely at the memory like a cat with the neck of a mouse. "No, do not fear suicide from me, Constance, any more than I fear it of you. We are angry American

women—we'll fight until the last breath, still wanting more than we ever had." She reached for my
hand. "Now be gone. I am tired, though I cherish
you, always."

When Katherine walked me to the door, she explained in her quiet deliberate manner that she feared
something new was truly amiss with Alice's health.
A small mass, like a stone, had begun to throb in the
left breast—yet Alice refused to mention this to her
doctor, believing it would dissolve if she drank the
proper balance of fluids. Katherine was determined
to win this battle.

So we all had our secrets.

That first year back in England I had rooms in the
village of Cheltenham, though I was to spend many
summer nights in King's London hotel, or in country
inns that we discovered together.

It had been five years since we'd seen each other,
and life had tested each of us. The lines of failure had
drawn their mark around his vibrant eyes; his thick hair
was licked with grey. I wondered how much stouter
and paler I seemed to him. He never said—other than
to yelp with joy at the sight of my plump self, stripped
of petticoats and drawers.

My new medical program was to involve something called artificial eardrums—a treatment that I had heard was extremely painful. I put off the contraptions until the autumn, so that I could give myself completely to my American visitor. Though I suffered the occasional attack during our time together, I never did confess to King that I had once succumbed to laudanum, and sometimes still felt its lure. I was afraid that in his unjudging worldiness he would simply go out and procure it for me rather than see me suffer.

Secrets. King had his share of secrets. There was his passion for dark-skinned women. John Hay was to tell me about it two years later, never suspecting why I cared so much about his mad geologist friend.

My friend King had many lives: the demanding Newport mother, who required constant financial and emotional support; the clandestine marriage to Ada Todd, the Negro woman who lived in Brooklyn and bore his children; the frantic urban life of clubs like the Players and the Knickerbocker, which bored him to tears. And then of course, the wild schemes, his desperate efforts to turn his knowledge of geology and exploration into money. He embarked on countless failed efforts to make a fortune as other men did, to be free from financial worry like his friends Adams and

Hay. Though I could see in him the erratic habits of the loner, the temperament of the dreamer rather than the businessman, my heart hurt for him all the same. Surely he deserved a streak of good fortune.

And where did I fit in? I cared not a wit. We talked and laughed and devoured each other like youthful sweethearts. I can only imagine what a picture we must have made, the grey-haired duo holding hands as we made our way through a Cotswold field, giggling through our kisses when a flock of sheep interrupted our path.

"I must find a buyer for this Idaho silver mine . . . the commission alone would solve all my problems," he said in our rooms in a Dorset inn one night. Empty plates sat on the dinner tray, a bottle of claret open on the dresser.

"You're not interested in Mexico any more?" I asked, swirling the remains of my wine glass.

"No. It's all about Idaho, now. The Mexicans are impossible to do business with . . . the men work like dogs but the authorities will hold you hostage for months on end. And the women are, by and large, too tired for anything once they're past the age of sixteen. Life is too hard."

"Good thing you know an American woman or two who've managed to stay energetic!" I laughed.

"You? You're better than ever. You are flourishing as you get older. Me, I'm just a burnt-out case of youthful promise gone bad."

"No, King, no—don't say that. I've had my own terrible times—betrayed by my body as well as people I love. The struggle never ends."

"I love you, Cons."

"I know, King." I kissed his calloused hands. "I can feel it."

"You should come home. Not to me, of course," he laughed. "But to America. You are an American."

"I am an American spinster, middle-aged."

"Not you, never." He grinned. "But haven't you had enough of it here? You've earned more than I've lost. Buy yourself a house. In the heat of Florida. You'd love it."

"You're not the first person to say that to me. My niece, of all people, actually planted the same idea when we were on our way to Cairo this spring." I sat up and untied my silk robe. "There was talk in my family of buying the house in Cooperstown that had been my grandmother's—as it came on the market for a good price. But I don't think I could bear the winters. It would have to be Florida."

"Or perhaps the Southwest . . . you would love that rugged red terrain," he said, slipping the robe off my shoulders and kissing the rise of my tired old collarbone as if it were a young girl's.

"I would love to see the desert, King, but for living, I need to be near the water." I unbuttoned his shirt and let my face rest in the fur of his chest. "Perhaps when I've completed these treatments for my ear, and finished my travels, I'll start to make plans for the great homecoming."

CHAPTER THIRTEEN

The Spoils of Alice

$\mathcal{I}$ bid farewell to Clarence King, not knowing if I would ever see him again. I never asked him where he was going next. Perhaps that is why we were so happy during our time together. Freed from the prospect of a future, I was able to drop the mantle of need and suspicion that I so often draped around myself. I was not flinching for the blow, waiting for him to hurt or disappoint me. And so he never did.

My energy turned once again to my work—and to my health. This mundane topic continued to draw the attention of my good friend Dr. Baldwin, who, like most sensible people, wintered in Italy. In the guise of serving as my cheerful Italian correspondent, he remained a constant presence in my English life. But interspersed with the stories of his boys and the gossip of the Misses Greenough and Murray and the minute observations of Florentine life, his letters always conveyed the same stalwart American message: discipline would save me.

How many times did I receive letters like the following:

My dear Constance:

Your perseverance is an inspiration to me—and, I trust, to you. What other proof do we require about the value of daily exercise in steadying the mind as well as the body? I say, walk in the rain, walk in the snow if you must—just wrap those fragile ears in fur and keep your spirits up.

Also, avoid sweets as they will only serve to enhance other appetites. No mixtures for you unless prescribed by me—we remain in agreement on that score, I trust.

As for missing Florence—do not romanticize the Italians so, as they are a childish people. Remember that when you left Bellosguardo, you were physically and mentally depleted. So it is not the only place where you can be happy. Yes, the view is lovely, the city enchanting—and you will see that all again, someday.

In the meantime, write us another story! And yes, I may take your advice on that score and begin to trace my own reminiscences.

Mrs. Baldwin sends her love.

The remarkable thing is that, for a long time, it worked. Once King departed, I surrendered to the English routine in all its local, village-bound glory. Combining Dr. Baldwin's dietary guidelines with my daily walks, I lost ten pounds. I wrote daily. I submitted to the trials of the artificial eardrums, small greased cotton pellets that I had to push into my ear canal with a contraption that looked like little forceps. The artificial drums were supposed to improve my hearing—though with no promise of relieving the pain, which was the greater burden. At times they actually caused such a shock of pain I wanted to scream aloud. But still, I refrained from taking any narcotics. Instead, I put the drums aside, read my Epictetus, wrote my letters, and pressed on.

I became a friend to my own thoughts, my own memories, once again. As long as autumn allowed, I rowed in the Avon, just as I had done in the Cayuhoga as a girl. When it became too cold, I would take a train

to one small village or another, make for the church or
cathedral, and stop for tea before heading home.

I saw a good deal of Harry, and even more of
Alice. The poor thing was diagnosed with breast cancer,
as Katherine had feared, in May of 1891. The great
performance of her life had begun.

That same spring, Clare and Clara, now the seasoned travelers, came through on their way to the
Continent. My sister Clara had it in her head that she
needed to experience Beyreuth, since Wagner was all
the rage back home. I declined to accompany them,
since my ears were no longer trustworthy companions
in my love of music. While my family scurried around
Europe, I moved my living quarters to Oxford. The life
of the university, the students, the river, the proximity
to London, all suited me far better than the remoteness
of provincial little Cheltenham.

It was one of my last moves, but it was a good
one.

Harry was a regular correspondent, though he was
consumed with the theatrical production of his book
The American. I confess I never quite understood why
this master of prose was so driven to prove himself as
a dramatist—though he claimed he wanted the chance

to earn "real" money, I often wondered if the real story was that some actor had captured his heart. Sharp-eyed Alice often joked that now she had something definite to die of, she would do her best to prolong the process so that her brother didn't have to deal with a real deathbed scene on opening night. The play had been touring the provinces throughout the year and opened in London one blustery October evening. Most people now know the story—the negative reviews, the efforts to revise and improve, the disappointing fifty-day run. But I don't think many ever knew how hard Harry took it.

He sent a note to say he needed to see me one grey November day. He arrived to find me in the parlor, reading another one of Dr. Baldwin's epistolary exhortations. Oriel Bill, the communal bulldog, sat at my feet, having learned that I was a soft spot for a long walk followed by a rewarding scrap or two from the table.

"Mr. James is here to see you, Miss Woolson, ma'am," announced Mrs. Beale, the landlady.

"Why Harry," I stood and extended my hand. "I've just been reading a letter from our friend Doctor Baldwin. He is such a taskmaster, even from Florence, that I'm beginning to think his talents are underutilized.

Perhaps he should travel around the world like Mr. Twain, selling his diet and exercise regime instead of humor."

Henry James stood looking around the stuffed English room, just as he'd done when he first came to call at the Pensione Barbensi so many years ago. Only now he was actually a bit thinner, and the grey worked through his hair rather than his suit.

"I wouldn't know, Fenimore. I'm certainly not one to gauge what the public wants to see or hear . . . as the current fiasco makes all too apparent. *C'est un desastre*."

He still didn't sit down. I took his hand and led him to an armchair by the fire.

"Harry, this will not do. We don't write for the critics. We write to tell the stories we want to tell—remember?"

"But I had already told this story, as a novel, and many thought it fine. That is why I thought it would be a success as a play."

"Stagecraft is a different art, Harry. You might as well say you decided to write symphonies or paint pictures. You have to give yourself the chance to learn how to do something you've never put your hand to before. Besides, I was there on opening night, amidst

the satin and the pearls, and I heard the applause despite
my weak ears. Many did love it."

"The applause of friends matters little compared
to the scorn of strangers. I don't think I have the courage to try again. I have lost my confidence."

"Life is not worth living at all without courage,
Henry. I hope I never outlive mine. You shall not outlive yours. Look at Alice for inspiration."

"Yes, but hers is a private struggle . . . my brother
William is a great success with his *Principles of Psychol-
ogy*, you know . . . yet I have not enjoyed true renown
since I published *Portrait of a Lady*."

I fought a wave of impatience with my friend.
Despite the hurts and the misunderstandings between
us, I had never experienced this sense of, well, mundane annoyance. His sister was dying; I could not hear
out of my left ear; and he was competing still with his
older brother. For shame, I wanted to cry.

"Harry, we do not write in order to win more rib-
bons in the school race than our siblings. We write—or
do whatever it is we need to do—because we must.
Because of the thing in itself." Bill moaned in assent
from my lap.

"Fenimore, is that a bulldog I see?"

"Yes." I dared him to ask why.

He pressed his lips together, tight. And then, at last, he laughed.

I scratched Bill's ear, shoved him to the ground, and stood up.

"Come Harry—I am going to show you the Baldwin cure for the blue devils. I warn you—it requires a hat and gloves. You are about to walk five miles along the Thames and tell me stories about what you see along the way. Just as we used to do, in Florence."

Henry of course was to have many more great performances in him. But that winter, Alice's only one lay before her.

Alice, many have said, had been dying her whole life. Yet that did not make her slow departure less terrifying for her, or those who loved her. Especially those of us who had looked in the mirror and spied there, for even one second, the reflection of our own mortality.

"Alice, it haunts me to think what you could have done if you'd been blessed with my strong Midwestern constitution," I said, sitting by her side one afternoon.

She gave one of those Alice caws that sounded like a little crow. "You don't fool me, Constance. To begin with: your roots are in New Hampshire and New York. So you're no more Midwestern than I."

I could have interrupted her with a story or two of Mackinac that would have shocked her Cambridge ears, but I held my tongue. Instead I just nodded.

"And you suffer from your own physical ailments. I can see it in your face sometimes—when the pain comes."

Trust Alice. Nothing escaped her.

"It is like a knife in my head," I whispered, confiding in her something I had never told her brother.

"So I thought." She stopped for a second. "You know, Katherine has been trying the new hypnosis with me, to relieve the pain. Sir Andrew Clark recommended it. Even Dr. Baldwin urged us to try, when he was last in town."

"I shall remember that, when I think that it might help me."

"I have been taking morphine to relieve the pain, at night, when it is too much," she paused. "Have you ever used it?"

"I did laudanum once, but it got the better of me," I confessed.

"Well, my dear, of course it did!" she cawed again. "Unless you want to be an opium-eater or one of those tragic laudanum-drinking females . . . it's not a medicine that can help one deal with anything over the long term. It is only suitable, I believe, when one is looking at a rather short period of time. As I am. Here we have a definite end point in sight." The branch of a tree scratched against the window, startling her. Then she fixed her eyes on me. "I have considered hurrying up that end point, when the pain is too much . . . but I cannot bring myself to ask Katherine for the killing dose."

"Better not to, I believe, Alice. Though I cannot say what I will do, when the time comes."

"Remember Constance—you and I are angry women. We must go out fighting."

Alice was the only person who ever told me I was angry. Was she wrong? Or uniquely prescient? I don't think I shall ever know.

Two weeks after that visit, on March 8, a package arrived at my Oxford quarters.

Inside there were two letters. One was a short note from Katherine Loring, telling me that Alice had passed away on March 6—news of which Henry had already telegrammed to me. What Henry hadn't mentioned was that as she lay dying, Alice had requested that Katherine read aloud to her my short story "Dorothy." This revelation was Katherine's gift to me. I was overwhelmed that my words were the ones that stubborn Alice wanted to hear as she left this world. My chest heaved with emotion. I put the paper aside so that my tears would not bleed the ink off the paper.

The other note was from Alice, as dictated to Katherine. It was marked "Private and Confidential" on the outside of the envelope.

My dearest Constance:

I know that you, more than anyone, will wonder what it feels like, at this moment—to accept, at last, that I won't be here to tell you all what it was like to die, after all this. *Strangely, it is a relief to look ahead and see: nothing. Though I could do without the flood of memories of people long gone—such as Mother and Father and my brother Wilky and that battle-axe old Aunt Kate. Why do they visit me, now?*

You have been a wonderful friend and inspiration to me. A woman who was not silenced by a pack of brothers, as I was. You seem to demand your place in the world, while remaining such a sympathetic and private person.

Many times I have been jealous of your friendship with Harry, and even tormented you (in the most girlish Bostonian fashion) about the nature of your attachment to each other. But now I see how alone he is, despite the frantic press of society. And so I want to give you my blessing.

Isn't that what you have always wanted? For me to say: yes, go ahead and marry him? I know that he asked you, once, in Switzerland. He confessed it to me. Remember: companionship is a stronger bond than sex—as I well know . . . You would help him so, calm him when the demons assault his spirit, keep his writing on track. And I like the idea of the two of you remembering me, fat and prosperous writers that you will be, in front of the fireplace. Perhaps you will write a tribute to me, together.

That would be a finer memorial than any headstone.

As always, your affectionate, Alice

CHAPTER FOURTEEN

The Blue Devils

*A*nd so Alice's final blessing was actually a curse. Not a curse in the sense that I was compelled to fulfill her wishes—which were, of course, easy enough to ignore—but a curse in the sense that nothing would be the same afterward. Whether she intended to or not, her morphine-laced letter had lifted a veil on an ugly truth I had worked so hard to ignore. That truth was, simply, this: my friend Harry was a selfish devil.

Did brother and sister actually plot and scheme together over the question of how to persuade good old Fenimore to become Harry's decoy wife? I doubt it . . . Harry was surrounded by willing women who would have been happy to be the kind of wife who turns a blind eye to a husband's extramarital pursuits, be they girls, boys, or circus animals. Besides, as a popular creative creature—an artist rather than an industrial magnate or a statesman—he had no need of such "cover."

No, I am certain that Harry simply mentioned the Swiss proposal to his sister in passing, in that deliberately casual way of his. Certainly they talked about it, briefly—after all, who would ever refuse a James anything, let alone a middle-aged spinster like me? My refusal must have puzzled Alice no end. But what angered me was his motivation. It was, simply, to control me. He just couldn't forgive me for having witnessed his *liaison dangereuse* on the terrace at Bellosguardo. And so rather than live in friendship, with the truth, he indulged in the fantasy that he could redefine us in a relationship that was a lie.

In short, he wanted to make me into a character in a Henry James novel.

Of course, I did not give him up. Not entirely. After all, I already loved him as he was. I still do. But I became wary.

Work, as always, would save me. I withdrew into the project of a new novel, set in the hills of North

Carolina. Though I had long wanted to place at least one of my longer fictions in Europe, I found myself in the grip of an intense homesickness. When my nephew sent me a photograph of his two children, with a smiling little sister "Constance," I felt a great yearning to see life anew through their young American eyes. I had never ached, as most women do, to have my own children—and I had always attributed my selfishness to those long years of tending to others, be they siblings or Mother. But now, perhaps, I was ready for the banal comforts—and demands—of home and family. I was no longer afraid of the time they would steal from me. Europe had accomplished what I wanted her to do. How wonderful if in my case, the dreaded "change" would be a freeing one.

So, in my long walks, I began to consider what it would mean to return to America. Could I summer in Mackinac or Cooperstown, and winter in Florida? I imagined the lemonaded splendor of an American summer day, golden grass and untrimmed trees shimmering in the late afternoon sun, and my spirits lifted. But perhaps I should see India first? Mr. Kipling had married the plainest of young American women, which tickled me no end. Such were my thoughts as I marched along the Thames, Oriel Bill by my side.

Until the return of my own blue devil. One afternoon, as I was nearing Oxford, the knife in my head sliced so hard that I lost my balance. The ground rose to meet me. Oriel Bill scurried round, licking my face. I lifted myself to a sitting position, and held my head in my hands. Not again, I moaned. Undergraduates glided by, laughing in their punts. An old tradesman stopped his cart in the road and asked if I needed help. When I explained that I was ill, he put Bill and me in his cart, and took us back to Beaumont Street. Every lurch of his old mare on the cobblestone street made me feel as if I were going to fly out of the wagon. But he was one of the kindest people I ever met.

The stab of the knife behind my left ear would never again subside, entirely. My true trials had begun.

At Dr. Baldwin's advice, I submitted to the care of a new doctor. However, the Oxford surgeon he recommended was no more empathetic than my Swiss doctor had been. Dr. Willow contended that my pain was purely "neurotic," which is, I believe, the new way of saying "neuralgic." But I knew even then that something physical—some inflammation or growth—had taken hold.

Dr. Willow insisted that I try a different kind of artificial eardrum—an Indian rubber disk on a fine silver wire, rather than the cotton pellet I'd used before. One tedious afternoon he must have inserted and removed the horrid thing fifty times, so that I could learn how to do it myself. Sitting in front of a mirror with my head dropped over my shoulder, the doctor's plump stomach pressing against me as he twisted the treacherous metal wire into my ear canal . . . it was a kind of hell. At last I sat up, asked him to step back, and took the wire from him. I guided it in myself, taking care to minimize the pain.

"Can you hear me now, Miss Woolson?" he shouted.

"Of course I can. I could always hear a single person speaking directly to me in a closed room," I answered.

"Wonderful," he exclaimed. "I knew these Toynsbee drums were the best."

I was charged to insert them every morning and remove them in the evening. Yet the wire was a cursed invader. With it, even the simplest move of my jaw sent a dizzying echo through my head. Chewing was agony. Talking, out of the question.

I returned to Dr. Willow's office, refusing to use them.

He turned and opened one of the many drawers in the cabinet behind him, and placed a small box on the table. "I'm happy to say I have an alternative—one made with a rubber stem instead of the wire. Some people do complain about the echo with the wire."

Why had we not begun with the rubber, I refrained from asking. He asked me to sit in front of the mirror again. It occurred to me that the rehearsal of the eardrum insertion was more for the doctor's sake than the patient's.

"Can you hear me now?" he shouted again.

"Yes, Dr. Willow."

"Excellent. You know, Miss Woolson, when I was a young surgeon, I had a patient who made an artificial eardrum for himself by rolling up a piece of paper into a little cylinder and wrapping it in cotton wool. When he inserted it into his ear canal, he was able to enjoy conversation at dinner for the first time in twenty years!"

"Poor fellow. Now what do you suggest I do about the pain, Doctor?"

It is amazing to me still how happy doctors are to prescribe narcotics to a fifty-year-old woman. I suppose they would do anything to keep us from talking. Our problems must bore them, to the core. But I kept my promise to Dr. Baldwin, and sent him copies of any new prescriptions from Dr. Willow for his approval. He allowed me one sleeping draught among the many offered.

The truth is, I seemed to spend every evening recovering from the supposed cures of my waking hours. The obedient patient, I made the tedious insertion of the eardrums part of my daily routine. Then one evening the rubber stem broke as I was trying to remove the drum. The result was agony—pressure building with the pain, mucous building. The rubber disk had to be removed by the surgeon with syringe and forceps.

I vowed never to use the wretched things again. And I telegrammed Dr. Baldwin to ask him to recommend a London physician. As long as I didn't have an attack at Paddington Station, London would be a welcome distraction. And so I found myself in the paneled chamber of the very kindly Dr. Brown.

"The eardrums are useless," he pronounced.

"That's what I've been saying."

"You do not suffer from a ruptured tympanic membrane."

"Excuse me?"

"Your eardrums are fine. Except of course for the inflammation caused by the renegade drum, which will subside. However, I would like to ask you some other questions . . . it is these seizures and falls that concern me."

For half an hour we talked about my dizziness, my spells, my vertigo. It is a doctor's role to comfort, to console, to assuage one's worst fears. Countless times over the course of a lifetime—at least, in my lifetime—it fell to a medical man to slay my darkest demons.

Therefore, it was fascinating—almost—to experience the reverse. Dr. Brown sat grimly across the sea of his leather-topped desk, his forehead gleaming with perspiration, his hands clasped tight, and told me that he believed a tumor was growing in my brain. And, that it was going to kill me.

"That's ridiculous," I said, becoming the doctor to his patient. "I've had pain in my ears for nearly twenty years now. It's not fatal."

"Whatever the cause of your original discomfort—be it infection or congenital malfunction, it only served to mask the earlier stages of the tumor. The dizzy spells, the pain, the mood swings, the seizure . . . quite frankly, Miss Woolson, I believe it's a miracle you've lived this long, on your own."

Cold crept through my body as he continued to speak. It occurred to me that I had a violent and sudden need to use the water closet. Cleveland girl that I was, I couldn't bring myself to ask him where it was.

"It gives me great sorrow to be the one to tell you this, Miss Woolson, but you will need to prepare. It may be months, it may be as long as a year. But you won't be able to live alone. At the end . . . well, the body will not be controllable."

I stared at his hands, clenched tight. "Will I be in pain?"

"I'm afraid so."

"Then I trust you will prescribe all the laudanum I need."

When I left his office, the street in twilight glowed. Every person shone like a firefly. Except that I was not chasing bugs with my sisters on Mackinac Island. I was on a crowded London street, the ornate buildings staunch with soot, the horses stinking in place as they waited for carriage traffic to move, men in dark coats and hats jostling me on the sidewalk.

I would not go home to be nursed. The realization that I might never see Florida again twisted the contents of my stomach. I bent over the curb and became ill.

But I would not stay here to die, either. I had to go south. And I had to see water.

CHAPTER FIFTEEN

Crossing

*H*ard to believe, but once I had absorbed the shock, a certain giddiness followed. Suddenly I had a reprieve from the minor oppressions of everyday life, such as next season's rent, and who was the new governor of Ohio, and who was going to marry whom when. It was like having a pass to be one's most selfish and unsocial self.

On the other hand, storytellers live in the future tense. All my life I had pulled myself out of low spirits by imagining what might happen next. Now there was not going to be any next. Everything needed to be experienced as it was. This was a test of my pragmatic soul.

"Like it or not, you must be a philosopher now, Connie," I wrote in my journal. I returned to Father's favorite Stoics, the ones whom Harry had once mocked. Now all I had was my own will and reason. I could not change the course of events; I could only handle them with dignity. Or in doing so would I in fact change the outcome? That was, and remains, my puzzle. For as soon as Dr. Brown gave me his terrible news, I experienced a relief in symptoms.

I would spend a few weeks in London while my possessions were packed up in Oxford and set off on the journey to Italy. I had a few days yet to decide between Venice and Florence as my destination. I sat on a bench in Hyde Park on a May afternoon—the kind of sudden warmth that draws everyone out from the woolen hibernation of winter—to contemplate what lay before me. The park sounded like an orchestra warming up with the sounds of children shouting and nannies calling and dogs chasing and birds singing.

Should I explain the cause of my sudden move to Harry, my sister, friends like John Hay? Then what would result . . . a flock of worried friends flapping their wings around me. Horror. If nothing else, I had permission to be selfish now. I would consult with Dr. Baldwin once I was settled in Italy. The others could wait.

And Harry, caught in the throes of grief—and guilt—over Alice. Harry would recoil from more female tragedy. Caught in the grip of his own blue devils, he was a frightening sight. The success of Hardy's *Tess of the D'Urbervilles* set him into such a jealous rage that he had to leave for Switzerland to calm himself. Presumably there were no tragic wanton dairymaids in the cool of the Alps.

A little boy ran back and forth in front of me. His laughter trilled like a cat our cook once had—happy cooing, like a bird. So loud that even I could hear it. No expert at guessing children's ages, I put him at five or six.

He chased a ball that a woman tossed to him. One strong throw sent it rolling beneath my skirts. Distraught, the child stopped in front of me, his face crumpled in confusion.

I reached beneath my skirts in most ungainly fashion and handed back the ball.

"Master Stephen," his nanny called, as she approached, "please don't touch the strange lady. Your mother will have my hide." Then she spirited her young charge away.

So that's who I had become. The strange lady. Three months before, I would have been the childless spinster moved to tears by the child she'd never had. Now I was the dying second-rate novelist, trying to decide where to spend her last days. Strange, indeed.

And who's to say that Dr. Brown is right, after all, I wondered, standing on the deck of the ferry for Calais. Though the spells had made a few quiet return visits, the channel was still not too rough for me. I held the rail with one firm hand and waved good-bye to England through the early morning mist that was already lifting in the June sun.

Harry had telegrammed from Switzerland, insisting that I wait for his return to London. But I had stopped waiting for other people the day my mother died. Now more than ever I needed to keep moving. And Paris would be my first stop.

It was there I began in earnest my catalogs. First was my catalog of favorite times—the moments I wanted to cherish throughout the year, and in my final breath, whenever it might be. Second, a catalog of my works, for my niece and for posterity.

I sat in the Café du Monde an odd sight indeed—a solitary middle-aged woman with an empty pot of tea and a plate of biscuit crumbs in front of her. I gestured to the waiter and asked for a glass of champagne. He smiled one of those tight French smiles and gave a little bow. I looked at my notebook.

1. *Hiking with Father in the foothills of New Hampshire, just the two of us.*

2. *Rowing in and around Mackinac the summer I was sixteen.*

3. *Graduating from Miss Chegaray's Finishing School in New York with honors and our celebratory lunch with Mama and Papa at Delmonico's.*

4. *Publishing my first story, "An October Idyl," in* Harper's *in 1870.*

The champagne arrived, together with a little dish of salted nuts. I stopped and took a long sip. It was dry and cool, just the way King liked it.

5. *Sitting in the Piazza della Repubblica in Florence with Harry, laughing, for the first time.*

6. *Lunch on the terrace of Villa Brichieri in Bellosguardo with Harry.*

Here I had to stop and breathe deep. Was the champagne going to my head? Impossible.

7. *The first advance check for* Anne.

8. *Dining with King in his rooms in Paris.*

9. *The wonderful reviews of* For the Major.

10. *Hiking with King in Cornwall and spending the night at the White Pheasant Inn.*

That's as far as I got.

CHAPTER SIXTEEN

Fairy Island

$\mathcal{I}$ stood beneath an umbrella, watching the porter and the gondolier heave the trunks onto the calle flanking the Casa Semiticolo. They had waved me inside, but I was determined to see that my belongings didn't slip into the green murk of the Grand Canal.

Harry used to say that packing for a trip was often more rewarding than the journey itself. I, on the other hand, always delighted in unpacking. Emptying the trunks, unfolding the clothes, arranging the books and the pictures, setting up house. It was for me the sign that a new project was about to commence.

When a book was done, I had to move.

But this Venetian unpacking was a melancholy affair.

I had spent the summer at my old favorite haunt, the Casa Biondotti, just near the Salute. But the ground floor was swarming with Cambridge Feltons and Nortons, a veritable Harvard seminar's worth. And I had set my heart upon a more dramatic dwelling on the Grand Canal. So when the crowds left in September, I moved to more glorious quarters. After all, there is no city more exotic than Venice, in all her watery splendor. And if I were choosing to stop here for my final, retrospective days, I would do it the way I wanted.

And what I wanted was to see the water. Everywhere.

I had placed my desk in one of the windows overlooking the Grand Canal. Now its crowded surface included the shabby mementos of every love affair: a program from the night act at Maxim's, the label from a bottle of Petrus 1877, a menu from the White Hart Inn in Dorset, a dog-eared photograph of my beloved King, leaning against a tall rock in the Sierra Nevadas before I had ever met him, the strong muscles of his thighs pressing through the fabric of his trousers. I picked up the photograph and kissed his beard.

What pathetic children we are, projecting so much meaning onto our paltry treasures, allowing them to become our memories. For a second I considered tossing them all in the bin. But I decided to set aside a copy of my manuscript for King, because of that promise Harry extracted that we would burn our letters to each other. I know if he finds this he will destroy it.

A letter arrived with the terrible news, now crumpled on the floor. The newspaper clipping fluttered in the breeze.

"Is Clarence King Insane?" read the headline from the *New York Sun*, dated November 3, 1893. My friend had attacked a Negro gentleman after making a scene at the Central Park Zoo, of all places. Rather than go to jail he'd checked himself into the Bloomingdale Asylum. King had scrawled across the top, "No more insane than Grover Cleveland or Henry Adams!" Hearing the cheer in his voice, I picked up the letter again.

Dear Cons:

Before they hauled me off to the madhouse, my Florida flamingo, I had not slept for two months . . . No excuse for trying to climb into the lions' den in the Zoo, I realize—but what's a fellow to do when even Wall Street's gone bust and matters of a domestic nature have bloomed beyond control?

Despair bites into and takes hold of that old back injury from the first Mexico expedition and tears into it with pointed teeth. No wonder I had to punish the lions who held me in their mouths like I was just a big old mouse. I needed them to loosen the bite. You understand, don't you?

Doctors don't know anything—my life is now only torture three times an hour, rather than every minute. But who is to say why? Am I simply used to the pain, or has the pain really abated? And then what relation does my mind have to my body? Which disorders the other? Which has the UPPER HAND?

So don't give up hope, my wild Michigan rose. You shall surprise all those waistcoated gents who trade in advice and potions. Science will save us all. Perhaps you should go to Vienna—I hear they are doing things with brains there. Then again, there is nothing like a true friend when you see him. Like me.

John Hay has been in Europe since July and no doubt told you many sad tales of the fiasco that is my life. He sends me checks every month, but does he approve of me? I think not.

Henry Adams, on the other hand, wants to take me to Cuba when I leave this place . . . since I love rum, primal woman, and heat, and he likes to watch.

You, my darling, are far more of a man than any of the Henrys in your life.

I do not believe that we shall ever die, you and I.

Your adoring and still reasonably sane, King

I walked on the Lido one last time, asked for my draught, and looked at the water. I had wanted easy access to the islands. Torcello, Murano, and most of all the Lido. Strange as it may seem, the Lido—that green island with its sweep of Adriatic-fronted hotels and wealthy tourists—reminded me of Mackinac Island. Not because the palazzi were anything like the large-porched American hotels, nor the cabanas and chairs like a lakefront American beach. No, the resort-ness of the place, its shadiness and boulevardy bonhomie (to sound like Harry) were a salve to my heart. I looked for licks of red maple, but they were not.

Only water, rising.

Epilogue

Venice, June, 1899

The heavyset man pulled at his waistcoat, which kept riding up over his stomach. It wasn't so easy to affect a casual, manly pose in a gondola, especially when the canal was so heavily trafficked. Truth was, it was much too warm for the London suit he was wearing. He dabbed his forehead with a square of linen while fixing his eyes on the consoling sight of the muscles that rippled in Tomaso's arms with each stroke of the pole.

He was stopping here in Venice again on his way back from Rome. He had visited her grave, at last, in the Protestant cemetery. Five years after her death.

"You had a terrible time here, Signor James, no? Maria and Josefina still talk about your lady friend. The one who died in the canal."

The American bristled at the idea of servants gossiping about him. But he could not erase the memory of those horrible days. He hadn't even gone to Fenimore's funeral in Rome. The scandal was too great. Suicide was grotesque.

But he had come to Venice a few months after her death, even stayed at her old rooms at Casa Biondetti, where she'd lived before moving to the Casa Semiticolo. He had to be there when the infernal sister and niece opened the box. What an ordeal it had been, weeding through the boxes and drawers and trunks, the shelves filled with books, the framed photographs of him and John Hay and Clarence King sitting proudly on her desk. She had been a pack rat until the end. He'd brought Fenimore's letter from all those years ago, after he'd published *The Aspern Papers*, when she'd agreed they would burn their letters to each other after death.

The sister and niece had wept, but allowed him to take the stack of letters clearly marked "Harry," tied in a separate bundle with the blue ribbon that had once been part of the silk pillow he'd sent her. He'd fed them to the fire, one by one, the brandy bottle open by his side.

How that fire had raged.

Thank God he'd found the damn manuscript. What had she been thinking? He'd thrown that in the fire too, page by sinister page.

It seemed that the fire would never go out.

Too much brandy. But he'd been so upset by the manuscript that he'd taken some of the dresses her niece had earmarked for the church. He'd run with them to the canal, where another beautiful rascal had rowed him out. The dresses had refused to sink. Black silk balloons, floating in the water. He'd grabbed the pole and stabbed at them.

It had taken him a long time to make them disappear.

Tomaso stopped the gondola in front of the Palazzo Barbaro, where his passenger was staying with the Curtises. "You okay, Mister James?"

"It was too bad, you see. Miss Woolson was a second-rate novelist, as most of the women are . . . the truth is, she wanted me to marry her." The old man reached out to touch the curls of the hopeful, hungry boy. "And we just couldn't face that now, could we?"

Tomaso grinned. "You want we go out to the Lido?"

Now this, thought the older American, will be something to cherish when I am back at Lamb House. For the rest of my life, I will adore water.

9